Was he searching for her?

Whatever he was doing, he was heading her way. Panting her fear, she clung desperately to control. Forcing herself to think, she tried to figure a way out. Visions of Suzanne lying on her bedroom floor caused a wave of nausea to rush through her.

Her world turned choppy, the survival instinct strong. Her eyes darted around the room.

Then she heard a thump. Vibrations. Marianna quickly moved toward the front door. It was locked.

Shaking hands fumbled with the dead bolt. Precious seconds ticked by as the key fell to the floor. The thumping stopped. She froze, her breath strangling her as she tried not to gasp.

Trembling, she bent down, snatched the key, jammed it in the lock and finally got the door open. She slipped out the opening, onto the porch, and felt hard hands grasp her upper arms....

Books by Lynette Eason

Love Inspired Suspense

Lethal Deception
River of Secrets
Holiday Illusion
A Silent Terror

LYNETTE EASON

grew up in Greenville, SC. Her home church, Northgate Baptist, had a tremendous influence on her during her early years. She credits Christian parents and dedicated Sunday School teachers for her acceptance of Christ at the tender age of eight. Even as a young girl, she knew she wanted her life to reflect the love of Jesus.

Lynette attended the University of South Carolina in Columbia, SC, then moved to Spartanburg, SC, to attend Converse College, where she obtained her master's degree in education. During this time, she met the boy next door, Jack Eason—and married him. Jack is the executive director of the Sound of Light Ministries. Lynette and Jack have two precious children, Lauryn, eight years old, and Will, who is six. She and Jack are members of New Life Baptist Fellowship Church in Boiling Springs, SC, where Jack serves as the worship leader and Lynette teaches Sunday School to the four- and five-year-olds.

A SILENT TERROR

LYNETTE EASON

Steeple
Hill®

Published by Steeple Hill Books™

STEEPLE HILL BOOKS

Steeple
Hill®

Recycling programs
for this product may
not exist in your area.

ISBN-13: 978-0-373-44331-4
ISBN-10:   0-373-44331-5

A SILENT TERROR

www.SteepleHill.com

Printed in U.S.A.

Keep me as the apple of your eye; hide me in the shadow of your wings, from the wicked who assail me, from my mortal enemies who surround me.
—*Psalms* 17:8–9

As always, to Jesus Christ. Let me be a good steward of what you've given me.

Thanks go out to:

The wonderful crime scene writers group on Yahoo. It's such a relief to know if I have a question, I can ask it and get an accurate answer in, sometimes, under a minute! You guys rock.

Emily Rodmell, editor extraordinaire. I'm honored to work with you. Thank you so much for taking a chance on a newbie and for making all my books shine.

Thank you to my deaf friends who are always eager to share their ideas, culture and language.

Thank you, dear hubby, for all the time and effort you put in to getting my books out there and for being proud of me.

Thank you, Lauryn and Will, I love you so much.

ONE

Something was wrong. Goose bumps pimpled on Marianna Santino's suddenly chilled flesh as she walked up her driveway. The door to her small home stood open. That in and of itself didn't bother her. The open door combined with the facts that it was January and slightly below freezing didn't bode well. And where was Twister, her large German shepherd, who normally bounded out to greet her?

Her internal fear alarm screeched. Adrenaline rushed.

Run. Get away.

She turned to run—and paused. But what about Suzanne?

Investigate or flee? What if Suzanne, her roommate, needed her? What if she was hurt?

What if whoever broke in was still in there?

Jamming her right hand into her coat pocket, she pulled out her Blackberry and punched in 911. When the screen lit, indicating the call was connected, she put the device to her ear to hear someone speaking. Unable to make out the words, she spoke softly into the phone. "Someone broke into my house." She gave the address and clicked off to wait. No doubt the dispatcher was probably yelling at her about hanging up, but it wouldn't do any good to stay on a phone with a person she couldn't hear.

Marianna scanned the house again. Her hearing aids picked up nothing out of the ordinary, just the wind whipping all around her, causing a whooshing sound to rumble in her ears. Other than that, all was quiet. Silent. Like a tomb.

Was the person still in there? Did Suzanne need help? Again the questions swirled in her brain, worry agitating her. Please God, don't let anything be wrong. Maybe the wind blew the door open.

But that didn't explain Twister's absence. And Suzanne, who always arrived home before Marianna, would have shut the door immediately.

Her eyes darted to the street. No police yet. Fear for her friend finally overrode her concern for her own safety. Slowly, she walked forward until she reached the front porch steps that led up to the door. The stain on the step stopped her.

Blood.

In the form of a shoe print. Leading out of the house.

She was beyond fear. Now she was terrified.

"Suzanne? Twister?"

Desperately, she strained for any sound that would penetrate the shroud of silence she lived with on a daily basis. With a shaking finger, she bumped up the volume on her hearing aid. Slowly, she stepped toward the door once more. The footprint led away from the house. That was good, right? Whoever had been there was now gone.

Or watching.

Glancing over her shoulder, she scanned the quiet street. After school normally meant children on bicycles and neighbors walking dogs. But the frigid weather had everyone inside. The street was deserted. Suddenly, the windows seemed ominous, staring back at her like empty eyes.

Where were the police?

Shivering, she stepped closer, avoided the bloody print and slipped inside the door. Looked down. Another print. A blast of warm air from the vent above her blew a lock of raven-colored hair across her eyes. Pushing it aside, she swallowed hard and made a concerted effort to control her fear-induced ragged breathing.

She continued on.

The kitchen to her right. Peered in. Nothing but an empty mug on the counter.

The den to her left. Again, nothing seemed out of place.

That left the three bedrooms down the hall. And the trail of bloody footprints leading to the room at the end.

With nerves taut, the hairs on her neck standing straight up, she took another deep breath and stepped into the hall, doing her best to avoid smudging the prints, which grew darker with each step.

Was she destroying evidence the police might need?

Hesitating, she chewed her lip. Her instincts screamed at her to get out. To leave.

But Suzanne might be hurt. What if she needed immediate medical help?

Those thoughts kept her going, ignoring the raging fear flowing with every heartbeat.

"Suzanne?"

A noise, caught by her hearing aid, pulled her to the left as did the prints. Suzanne's bedroom. The door was shut.

Reaching out, she almost touched the knob. Stopped. Every crime show she'd ever watched seemed to replay through her mind in a five-second span. She caught the edge of her shirt, gripped it with her thumb and pointer finger, and twisted the knob to open the door. No sense in marring any fingerprints that might be there.

No, you're just possibly wiping them off.

But Suzanne was her priority.

Another muffled sound. What was that? Run!

Please, God!

The knot in her throat grew tighter as the door swung inward. A bloody smudge marred the hardwood floor. And another one just behind it. The room lay trashed, items broken and strewn about.

Oh, please, Jesus, let the police get here soon.

"Suzanne? Twister?"

Another sound. From the closet. Slowly, she walked toward it. Using her shirt again, she grasped the knob and turned it.

The door exploded open, pushing her backward to land on her rear. She let out a little scream, then groaned.

Twister. Licking her face, he expressed gratitude for his freedom.

"Get off. Down," she ordered.

Immediately, he dropped to his haunches, ears perked, brown eyes gleaming. Cocking his head, he whined, seemed restless, his attention on something beyond her bed.

She whirled, rounded the bed and stopped.

"No!" she screamed and dropped to her knees.

Suzanne lay faceup, eyes fixated, unseeing, on the ceiling above her. Beneath her dark hair, a pool of blood soaked into the light brown carpet.

As Ethan O'Hara approached the house, the scream reverberated from within. The wide-open door and the brown bloody footprint on the front porch told him that the 911 hang up call signified real trouble. Definitely not a prank. Catelyn, his partner, pulled her gun and gave him the nod; he entered the house, his own weapon held ready in his right hand. They'd been passing by the neighborhood when the scanner went off. When Catelyn heard the address, she gasped, "That's Marianna's house, I think."

"You know her?"

"I'm better friends with her sister, Alissa, but I've met Marianna a couple of times."

Instead of waiting for a unit from the county, he and Catelyn had simply made a right turn into the subdivision, calling in that they would handle it.

She followed behind him, covering his back. Silently, senses on high alert, he tracked the prints.

Again he heard, "No!" coming from the back bedroom on his left.

Not wanting to call out and possibly alert the perpetrator who could still be around, he controlled his breathing, felt the familiar rush of adrenaline he always had going into a potentially dangerous situation and stepped into the bedroom.

The bed sat centered on the opposite wall. Sobs came from the right of it. He took in the debris-littered room. Someone had put up a violent fight. Catelyn came up behind him indicating the rest of the house was clean.

Lowering his gun to his side, he met her eyes, then turned back to see a woman lying on the floor beside the bed, her head resting in a stain of red. The crying came from the other woman who knelt at the figure's side, long dark hair hiding her face.

"Ma'am?"

No response.

"Ma'am?" He touched her shoulder.

She jerked, screamed and scrambled sideways. Movement to his right brought him around and face-to-face with a German shepherd, whose sharp teeth, bared in a snarl, looked capable of tearing Ethan's throat out.

"Easy, boy," he soothed, backing up a step, flashing his badge to the scared woman trembling just out of reach.

"Twister, no. Sit," the woman commanded, her voice clogged with tears.

The snarling stopped. The dog sat, popped a yawn, then, with his tongue lolling out of the side of his mouth, grinned up at Ethan.

Breathing a little easier, Ethan was able to turn his attention back to the body on the floor...and the woman whose liquid ebony eyes flicked between him and Catelyn. Catelyn moved over to see the action this side of the bed. In a gentle tone, she said, "Marianna, it's me, Catelyn, Alissa's friend. This is my partner, Ethan O'Hara. What happened?"

Marianna blinked, swiped a few stray tears and gave a shuddering sigh. "Oh, Catelyn. I...I don't know. I just...came home from work and found...this...her. The front door was open and...I called 911, but couldn't wait for help. I had to make sure she was all right, but...she's not."

Another muffled sob, more silent tears.

No, the woman definitely wasn't all right. The coroner would need to make a trip out here. Ethan asked, "Who is she, your sister?" They looked enough alike.

A negative shake caused her hair to shimmer, a few strands stuck to the salty tracks on her cheeks. She brushed them aside. "My roommate. Suzanne Miller."

Twister crawled over to rest his head on his mistress's knee. Her slender fingers buried themselves in the animal's silky fur.

"Who are you?" he asked.

He knew Catelyn could fill him in, but he wanted to know now. He told himself his wanting to know was strictly professional and had nothing to do with the fact that she was probably the most gorgeous woman he'd ever laid eyes on. He blinked, forcing himself to focus on her words, not her looks. Or the sound of her voice, which had an accent he couldn't quite place.

Marianna glanced at Catelyn, then looked back at him. She said, "I'm Marianna Santino. I teach at the Palmetto State School for the Deaf across the street."

The deaf school. He'd refused to acknowledge it as they'd passed it on their way to this subdivision. His sister had gone to school there for many years. It held a mixture of bittersweet and painful memories for him.

Looking straight at her, he said, "I hate to tell you this, Ms. Santino, but it looks like your roommate either surprised the perp...or he was after her and caught her." He looked around, then motioned to Catelyn. "We need to get out of here. This scene's been contaminated enough. Call it in and secure the area, will you?"

Catelyn went to do as he requested. Ethan held his hand out to the woman.

"But everyone loves Suzanne," Marianna protested even

as she accepted his helping hand. Twister stayed right beside his mistress. "She teaches kindergarten at Pine Wood Elementary School."

"Well, it looks like she made someone really mad about something."

Marianna missed that last part; he'd turned his head and she'd not been able to read his lips. Something about someone being mad. But who?

She followed him from the room, down the hall and out the door. What had Suzanne stumbled upon? Had she been up there all day, or had she come home early from work?

A hand on her arm brought her attention back to the man before her. His concerned blue-gray gaze narrowed, zoomed in on her. For some reason she noticed the touch of gray at his temples. "Oh, I'm sorry. You said something. I was thinking, picturing poor Suzanne…" She bit her lip. He didn't need her to break down again. He needed her help.

"Are you with me here?"

"Yes, yes, I'm sorry." She really needed to stop apologizing. None of this was her fault. "I'm almost deaf and need you to face me when you talk to me so I can read your lips, all right?"

Understanding flashed across his rugged features. The flicker of pain she glimpsed on his face confused her, but then it was gone and he was all business. "I need to ask you some questions, all right?"

Marianna nodded. Probably the same questions she had running through her mind. They walked to the curb, Twister trotting beside her.

Ethan asked, "Does Suzanne have any enemies?"

"No, like I said, she teaches…taught…kindergarten."

"A fight with a boyfriend?"

"She doesn't have a boyfriend right now. She recently broke up with a guy named Bryson James, but it was amicable."

He jotted something in the small notebook he had pulled out. When he looked up, his electric gray-blue gaze connected with hers again and she felt a pull, sensed comfort, strength...a hidden pain?

She jolted, not wanting to feel anything right now or notice the good-looking cop sitting on her couch. Suzanne was dead, and the police needed her full attention to help solve her murder.

"Family?"

Marianna rubbed her hand across her forehead, swallowing another wave of grief. She whispered, "Her parents live here in town. They'll be devastated." He shifted next to her. She stared helplessly at him. "What can I do? How do I help?"

His big calloused hand reached over to take hers, his gaze intense as he said, "You're helping in just answering the questions. Don't leave anything out, tell me everything you know about her. The smallest detail could wind up being the biggest clue, okay? Then we're going to have to find you a place to stay for a couple of days until we can release the scene—" he cleared his throat "—um, your house, back to you."

Marianna nodded and sucked in a fortifying breath, and for the next hour and a half, while officers, a CSI unit, the medical examiner and the coroner paraded through her home and Suzanne's privacy, she did her best to give Ethan O'Hara something to work with to enable him to find Suzanne's killer.

Ethan waited while Marianna sent a text message to her parents that she would be coming to stay for a couple of nights. He was glad texting was such an in thing these days, since it made communication so much easier for the deaf. His sister would have loved the technology. Instead of dwelling on the past, however, he focused on what the crime scene investigator was saying.

"The medical examiner ruled out suicide. Ms. Miller was killed when she cracked her head on the corner of the bedside table. Blunt force trauma, if you want the official term. The M.E. said she'd do an autopsy to be sure, but she doubted she'd find anything else."

"I'll talk to her later. Thanks for the help and let me know if you find anything else, will you?"

"You bet, Ethan."

Marianna walked toward him, her beauty not one bit diminished by her puffy eyes, red nose and blotchy cheeks. The grief stamped on her face pierced him. Why was it always the good ones? The ones who didn't deserve to have their lives shattered this way? Not that anyone *deserved* to come face-to-face with murder, but…

Melancholy thoughts would haunt his after-hours work tonight. He smirked at that thought. What after-hours? As a homicide detective, he lived his job twenty-four/seven. Maybe if he had a family, someone to go home to at night, he'd make more of an effort to work less and spend time at home.

He smiled at her and noted the well-trained Twister at her side. Ethan commented, "He reminds me of the dogs on the K-9 squad."

Tilting her head, she grinned. His heart slammed against his chest, and his breath whooshed from suddenly constricted lungs. Wow. Twin dimples flashed at him as her eyes crinkled at the corners. "Twister is a special dog, specially trained to be my ears. I don't know what I'd do without him."

Then the dimples disappeared, the brief moment of levity gone. It shocked him to realize how much he wanted her to smile again. "Do you need a ride to your parents' house?"

"No, but thank you. My brother, Joseph, is on the way to pick me up. He's home, visiting. My mother let him know I needed a ride, but she didn't tell him why." Her hands clasped in front of her, she kept her eyes on his face. She looked lost, shell-shocked.

The urge to gather her in his arms singed him. Instead, he cleared his throat. "Why didn't she tell him?"

Well-shaped shoulders lifted in a shrug. "A lot of reasons. The main one being the safety of the other drivers on the road between her house and mine."

"Right. Okay, well, there's nothing else we can do here."

He placed a hand on her shoulder, felt a tremble run through her.

Don't do something dumb, O'Hara, like hug her.

He pulled her to him for a brief moment, patted her back, then stepped back. The surprise on her face matched the disbelief he felt. He'd hugged her. Now why did he go and do that? What was it about her that had him tossing his professional detachment to the wind? She offered him a small smile filled with gratitude.

Swallowing his rampant thoughts and emotions, he realized he'd only just met the woman and was getting in deep, reacting with his heart, instead of his head. Clearing his throat, he said, "Hey, it'll be all right. Everything will work out, okay?"

Unblinking identical vats of chocolate stared up at him.

Her eyes made him think of Hershey's—and kisses...and not necessarily the candy kind. She asked, "Will I see you again?"

"Oh, yeah, I think that's definitely going to happen." He didn't realize he'd spoken the words aloud until he watched the flush rise from her neck to her cheeks.

Oops.

Catelyn stomped the mud off her shoes, diverting his attention from the woman in front of him. When he looked to the door, Marianna did likewise.

His partner said, "I've questioned all the neighbors I could find." Her lips twisted in disgust. "Nobody saw anything. Her next-door neighbor was home from work with the flu. Said he heard a crashing sound sometime this morning but felt too bad to get up to see what it was."

Ethan's eyes sharpened, "Probably that trash can that was overturned. Check that out to make sure he didn't dump anything."

A car turned into the drive. He turned back to Marianna. "I think your ride has arrived."

Marianna winced. "You mean trouble has arrived."

TWO

How was she supposed to go back to a normal life? Marianna had taken off yesterday and the day before, calling in sick and staying at her parents' house, she and Twister fortunate enough to be wrapped up in her mother's love and concern. Now it was Friday morning and she was on her way to the school. According to Suzanne's mother, the autopsy had been finished and her funeral was tomorrow.

But, first, Marianna had to make it through today. She'd chosen to go to work instead of sitting around thinking about the brutal loss of her friend, so she was expected to teach without falling apart. But how? *My strength is in You, Lord. Please get me through this day.*

The day of the murder, Joseph, her eldest brother, had picked up her and Twister up from her small house and taken them to her childhood home, drilling her like a dentist for the entire ten-minute drive. When she'd said trouble had arrived, she should have said the Spanish Inquisition had been *revived*.

She chalked it up to his being an FBI agent and the boredom of vacationing having set in. And the fact that someone had just killed his baby sister's roommate. Concern came naturally for him, overprotectiveness his first instinct. One of the reasons her mother hadn't told him about the murder when she'd ask him to pick her up. Joseph could handle just about any situation with a coolheaded professionalism except when it came to his baby sister.

It drove her nuts.

Throughout her entire childhood and most of her adult years she had fought to prove she could take care of herself and to get her family to stop hovering simply because she was deaf. She was just glad Joseph had agreed to go get her car yesterday afternoon. Being stuck without transportation made her feel trapped, like a bird with clipped wings.

She'd snuck out this morning, avoiding her mother's delicious-smelling breakfast. When she'd considered eating, her stomach had lurched in protest. The only thing she'd been able to force down yesterday had been soup and some fruit.

As the school building came into view, she glanced across the street at the entrance to her neighborhood. Would it hurt to drive by? Just to see? A quick glance at the clock told her she'd be late if she did. Resisting the urge to spin the wheel to the right, she entered the campus. Waving to the guard at the entrance, she made her way down the road, cut a right into the first parking lot she came to and whipped into an empty spot.

The building where she taught sat up on a hill. A big hill. Unfortunately, some brilliant architect had designed the nice building but neglected to add a parking area anywhere near it. Hence the lower-level parking and the breath-stealing hike to her classroom.

At least she got her exercise every day. Grabbing her ever-present backpack from the passenger seat of her car, she slammed the door and began the ascent. Other staff members were in the process of arriving and several waved.

"Marianna!"

She turned at the sound of her name. Julie had obviously been calling it a few times as the woman rushed up to her, panting, bending over to catch her breath. "I keep forgetting you can't hear people yelling at you."

Marianna laughed for the first time since Suzanne's death.

Julie Thomas, friend and fellow teacher, could always be counted on to produce a smile. "Nope. You just have to hit the right pitch. How long have you been calling me?"

Julie shot her a dark look. "Long enough." A frown knitted her blond eyebrows together. Sucking in a deep breath, she said, "Okay, I can finally breathe again."

She waved toward the hill they still had to climb. Fortunately, some bright soul had taken pity on the Green Hall staff and had built steps into the side of the hill. Marianna headed for them, watching Julie's lips and listening intently as her friend asked, "Are you all right? I mean, I can't believe someone broke into your house and killed Suzanne. It's just…"

"Insane?" Marianna asked quietly.

"Yes. That's the only word for it." Thankfully, while Julie had her funny side, she could be serious when the time called for it. Marianna felt Julie's hand on her arm. She stopped walking and looked around into her friend's green eyes, which held a sheen of compassion-induced tears. "Truly, are you all right?"

Sighing, Marianna leaned over to give the concerned woman a hug. "No, I'm not all right yet, but with God's help and by finding Suzanne's killer, I will be," she whispered. "I have to be."

They finished the walk to the two-story building in silence. Julie went to the bottom floor, which contained the middle school. Marianna went upstairs to the multi-handicapped school. The middle school students were on an academic track that would prepare them for college. The students in the multi-handicapped school were on the occupational track. They would find themselves with a job suited to their needs and live either with family or in a group home.

And while their IQs might not be the highest, they still had a great love for socialization. In fact, most of her students were just like any other teenagers, discussing the current television programs and the newest dance, and using the latest technology to communicate with each other. The school was a great place and Marianna loved it.

She greeted the secretary with a smile. "Hi, Jean."

"Oh, you poor girl." All five feet two inches of Jean Witherspoon ejected from behind her desk, and she rushed over to give Marianna a maternal hug. "What on earth happened? Has there been any word on who...well, any more developments?"

No one wanted to say the word *killed* or *murdered*. Marianna certainly didn't want to either read the words on peoples' lips or hear them with the help of her hearing aids. No, she'd rather avoid both words.

She shook her head. "No, nothing. I'm hoping to hear something soon."

"Are you going to be okay? Do you think you can concentrate today?"

Leave it to Jean to cut to the heart of the matter. "No, probably not, but I'm going to give it my best shot."

A pat on her arm pulled her attention to the boy standing next to her. Actually, the word *boy* wasn't exactly accurate for this student, Josh Luck, who was six feet four inches tall and would normally be called a man if it weren't for the fact that he had the mental capacity of about a five-year-old. At twenty-one years old, he would "age out" and graduate in five months. His handicapping label also read "autistic," but he had a mild form of it, because he enjoyed hugs and physical touch.

And he loved to bring her gifts. Specific gifts.

Just about every day Josh would bring her some new computer piece from his seemingly endless supply. She'd talked to his father about it and the man just laughed it off, told her to throw them out or whatever. Josh had so many computers and parts at home that there was no way to keep up with it all. If the boy wanted to give her something, he obviously didn't think he'd need it. But each week she would send the parts home...just in case.

Josh was also known as a savant. He knew how to take apart a computer down to the last screw and put it back together almost with his eyes closed.

He was going to have a great career in computer repair...with a little help from the school-to-work transition team.

Marianna said, "See you later, Jean. I need to see what Josh's brought me today."

She led Josh down the hall to the third classroom on the right. He followed her and tapped her shoulder again. Marianna shook off her coat and hung it in the closet. Josh waited patiently.

Then she turned and held out her hand, palm up.

Josh placed a computer piece in the center of it, then clomped off to sit in his specially designed desk. His lumbering, bulky frame had decimated several regular student desks before the maintenance department workers finally took it upon themselves to build him an indestructible one. So far, so good.

Several more students made their way into the classroom, stopping for their morning hug and encouraging word.

The single wooden door to her classroom suddenly seemed to morph into a revolving one. One by one, other teachers and staff stopped by to express concern and condolences. Marianna kept a smile on her face and the tears at bay by sheer willpower.

It wasn't until she placed her purse in the bottom drawer of her desk that she realized something seemed...off. She turned to her assistant, Dawn Price, and said, "Did you move things around on my desk?"

Forty-five years old and a veteran assistant, Dawn looked up from where she'd been asking a student about his morning. "No, why?"

Marianna looked at the small potted plant that normally sat on the back corner of her desk. It had been moved up closer to the edge above the drawer. Her stapler was on the left side instead of the right. Several papers she'd stacked neatly looked as if they'd been rifled through.

She shook her head. "Things just aren't where I left them."

She shrugged. "Maybe the cleaning crew had to move my desk and things got shifted."

Soon, a student had her attention and she focused on getting through the morning.

Praying the day would end soon, she did her best to concentrate on the students, pouring as much as she could into their eager minds.

Ethan threw the pen down on the report and rested his head in his hands.

"What's wrong, partner?" Catelyn asked as she found a perch on the side of his desk.

"This case," he mumbled into his palm.

"Yeah." Confusion colored her voice. "I don't understand the complete lack of evidence."

He snorted and looked up. "We've got evidence, such as the shoe print, it just isn't leading us anywhere. The fact that there were no viable fingerprints leaves us cold. Not even a stray hair. I don't get it. Suzanne put up a struggle—didn't she? The room was torn apart."

"There's no indication she fought back." Catelyn dropped a sheaf of papers on his desk. "The M.E.'s report. Nothing under her fingernails, nothing on her clothing."

"Then she surprised him. The room's not trashed, because she fought him, he trashed it before she got there." Tapping his chin, he looked at the papers but didn't pick them up. "He wasn't expecting anyone to be there."

"Okay, so he broke in, started gathering his loot in the bedroom, was there maybe a couple of minutes when Suzanne walked in on him."

Nodding, Ethan said, "She startled him and he grabbed her, she probably would have pulled back, maybe stumbled and fell, hitting her head? Or maybe he pushed her trying to get out of the room. I don't know, just speculation, but..." he said, shrugging.

"But where was her car? The one in the driveway was registered to Marianna. And it was clean. No sign of a search or tampering."

His gaze snapped up to hers. "You're right. There was only Marianna's car. The garage was empty."

"Suzanne may not have owned one."

"One way to find out." A few taps onto the computer keyboard brought up a number of Suzanne Millers in the Spartanburg area. He scrolled down to the right one listing her address and clicked. Suzanne's pretty features as shown on her driver's license filled the top right corner of the screen. Finding the area of the screen he wanted, he clicked again.

She owned a black Honda Accord. Glancing up at Catelyn, he pointed to the monitor. "Look."

Catelyn looked at him. "So, what are you waiting for?" She glanced at the clock on the wall opposite his desk. "It's twelve forty. I've got another appointment, but it's plenty of time for you to be waiting on Marianna when she walks out of class. Actually, she's probably at lunch. It's Friday, so the buses start picking up the kids at one." The residential school dismissed the students early on Friday because some of the kids had a four- to five-hour trip home. The drivers and attendants who staffed the buses stayed the weekend in whichever city was at the end of their route, then brought the students back on Sunday night.

"Yeah, I know the schedule." Without another word, Ethan grabbed his coat and headed out the door.

Fifteen minutes later, he'd flashed his badge to the guard at the entrance and refused the offer of directions to the building called Governor's Hall, the cafeteria where the students gathered each day to eat, then stand outside to wait for the buses. He knew the way.

Ethan now sat outside the building watching the end-of-day activity. Two high school boys tossed a football with one hand and signed back and forth with the other, talking in a language Ethan had done his best to forget, yet remembered with no trouble. Another young man stole a kiss from the girl he held hands with as they strolled up the hill toward the area where they would wait for the bus to pick them up. A group of elementary students crossed the street at the crosswalk, and a little girl about seven years old stooped to entice a cat to come to play until she was hurried on by the worker bringing up the rear.

Nothing changes, he thought. When his sister had been a student here a little over three years ago, the same two boys played football, the same couple held hands—everything was the same. Then he shook himself. Of course everything wasn't the *same,* but it sure did bring back memories.

Memories that brought the pain of his sister's death to the surface one more time, along with the resentment of his parents' just moving on as if nothing had happened, as if his world hadn't been ripped apart. A week after her funeral, his parents had left to tour Europe. Sure, they'd asked him to go with them, but he'd been shocked at their plans, had thought they were crazy, insensitive, unfeeling.

Forcing his thoughts from the past, he concentrated on watching for the one person he hadn't been able to push from his mind.

Marianna Santino.

And then there she was. Coming out of the cafeteria, her heavy wool skirt swaying against her endless stretch of legs. The baby-blue, cable-knit sweater only enhanced her dark beauty. She had her raven-colored hair flowing around her shoulders and down her back, just as she had two days ago.

His palms suddenly itched, curious to feel what it would be like to let that hair flow through his fingers. Curling his traitorous hands into fists, he told himself to focus. He was here on a case, not a date.

And soon she would be gone from his sight. Where was she going? Climbing from his car, he followed her. She was on her BlackBerry, texting someone, her fingers flying over the keys. Totally focused on her task, she kept her head down, never looking left or right—not exactly the best defensive walk. But then she wasn't the one who needed to be on the defensive; Suzanne was the one who'd been killed.

He wondered how Suzanne had walked. Probably like Marianna, completely unaware of her surroundings. The thought chilled him.

"Marianna!"

She didn't turn. Instead, she flipped her phone shut, pulled open the glass door and slipped inside the building. Closing in fast, Ethan saw her enter the third classroom on the right.

Reaching the door, he entered after her. Her desk faced the door and she stood behind it, pulling a box from a drawer. "Marianna?" He moved farther into the room.

Looking up, she gasped. "Oh, Detective O'Hara."

"Sorry, I didn't mean to startle you. And it's Ethan."

"Ethan, then. And it's all right." She held up a shoebox. "I'd forgotten to give this to Josh to take home last Friday, and with all the craziness *this* week, I forgot to give it to him today. He loves to bring me computer parts each week. I believe in recycling, so I was just going to rush down to the bus pick-up area and give it to him."

"Come on, I'll drive you. I've got a few questions to ask if you don't mind."

She blew out a sigh, grief crossing her flawless features for a brief moment. She shut the drawer and walked around the side of the desk. "I don't mind. I can't think of anything I haven't already told you, but maybe your questions will jar something."

Together, they walked back to his car, with Marianna greeting various staff and students along the way. When they reached his vehicle, he drove her around to the where the buses picked up the students and she hopped out. Ethan stayed put and watched her approach an on-duty staff member. She asked in sign language while voicing, "Cleo, has Josh already gone?"

Cleo signed back, "Yes, his bus left about five minutes ago."

Marianna sighed, hands gracefully forming the words,

"Oh well, it wasn't anything major, just his box. I guess I'll save it for next week."

"You want me to keep it until Monday? I have to go back to my classroom anyway, so I don't mind."

"Sure, thanks." Marianna handed over the box of treasures with a dimpled smile, then walked back to climb in Ethan's car. "Do you want go up the street to the coffee shop to talk?"

"Sounds good to me."

The sooner he got this investigation out of the way, the sooner he could start thinking about asking Marianna Santino out on a date. Maybe. If he thought his heart could handle it.

Ice Cream and Coffee Beans, home to tasty milk shakes and fresh-brewed coffee. Sandwiches could be ordered, too. Marianna chose a peanut butter shake with whipped cream. Ethan decided on a chocolate one, sans the white topping, and a club sandwich.

A plain, no-frills kind of guy, she thought. Nice. He kept his beard trimmed close and his mustache neat. A well-shaped mouth with firm lips smiled at her through the facial hair. Sometimes it was hard to read the lips of people who hid them behind beards and mustaches, but not Ethan. He was an easy read. His lips anyway; his eyes were another story.

He said, "I can't believe you went to work today."

Taking a sip of her milk shake, she relished the sweet richness on her tongue for a minute before swallowing. "I had to." She leaned back against the booth. "I love my parents, and my mom would like nothing better than for me to come home on a permanent basis, but one day was enough." She gave a wry smile. "And Joseph was driving me nuts."

"Your brother?"

She nodded, admiring the breadth of his shoulders, the strength that he exuded. "He's an FBI agent who works in New York. He works a lot of missing person cases. It's the first time he's been home in almost a year, and he gets confronted with this. I told him to stay out of it, but don't be surprised if you get regular calls for updates from him."

"Not a problem."

Sucking in a deep breath, she asked, "So, what kind of questions did you have?"

"Catelyn and I were hashing over the case and we realized there was only one car in the driveway—yours. Where's Suzanne's?"

Marianna furrowed her brow. "Oh, I'd forgotten all about that. It's in the shop getting new brake pads. She was supposed to pick it up yesterday. Since we live so close to my school, I let her use my car to drive to work and I just walked." She rubbed a hand across a forehead that was beginning to ache. "I'll have to call her parents and let them know to go get it."

"I'll take care of that. I also called Suzanne's school. They said she arrived on time Tuesday morning and signed in but left early because she was sick. We do know that she signed out at four minutes after ten. Assuming she didn't stop anywhere because she felt bad and wanted to get home and go to bed, I think it's safe to say she probably arrived home around ten-fifteen. The murder happened shortly after that."

Grief cut into Marianna. She didn't want to think about it anymore but was determined to do whatever it took to catch Suzanne's killer.

Running a hand over her hair, she smoothed it down around her ears, a habit she'd picked up two years ago. Curt Wentworth, her ex-boyfriend, hadn't wanted to see her hearing aids. They made him self-conscious and uncomfortable. Which was really strange, since he'd chosen audiology as a profession. She hadn't realized until too late that his constant stroking of her hair hadn't been out of affection; he'd been covering up her hearing aids. Marianna sighed. No use thinking about him.

Forcing her thoughts away from Curt's unpleasant memory, she focused on an awful thought. "So, Suzanne came home sick and walked in on a burglary. He killed her and ran."

"That's what it looks like."

Tears choked her, blurring her vision. She blinked, refusing to let the endless tears fall. "She should have stayed at work," she whispered.

His hand covered hers, and she shivered at the contact. It had been a long time since she'd been attracted to a man; she had been a little gun-shy since she and Curt had broken up six months ago. Her surprising feelings scared her and yet...

She watched his mouth and focused on his words. "Yes, if she had she would probably be alive. But, she didn't and..." he sighed, then looked up at her. "Was Suzanne a Christian?"

That question startled her. "Yes, she was."

"Then there's comfort in that, right?"

Marianna relaxed a fraction but nodded and offered a feeble smile. "Yes, of course, but I, and everyone else who loved her, will miss her." Tears gathered again. She sniffed, grabbing up the napkin with her free hand to dab her eyes.

"I know." His fingers squeezed. Marianna started at the tingle that raced up her arm. Trying to be discreet, she pulled her hand from his and picked up her milk shake. The sparkle in his eye said she hadn't fooled him.

But now wasn't the time to pursue the mutual attraction. Marianna had a funeral to attend, and Ethan had a murder to solve.

Feet thudded against the stairs, phones rang, voices raised in argument filled the air. The person seated at the desk ignored the chaos coming from the room to the right. "Where have you been?" Tense fingers gripped the phone as the frantic voice shook, wobbled, fought for control and said, "I had things to take care of. The girl's dead. She surprised me. I didn't mean to kill her. She fought back and I pushed her...."

"Do you know what you've put me through having to

explain your absence? Look…never mind. So, you didn't find it."

"No." Harsh, frantic breathing.

"Calm down. We have to have it. If the wrong people get their hands on that…everything we've worked so hard for is down the toilet." A string of curses rent the air.

"I know, I know. But she probably doesn't even realize what she has."

"Doesn't matter. If she looks at it…"

"I can't do this. If anyone finds out, if I get caught, our careers are finished. I can't believe this. I never meant for…" A frustrated sigh sounded, then, "Let someone else do it. I can't."

"Are you crazy? The last thing we need is someone else involved. Right now, the only people who know about this are you and me. We need to keep it that way. This is your fault. If I have to come up there and take care of this…"

"I know, I know. Maybe I should just go to the police…explain that it was an accident."

A harsh laugh echoed. "What fantasy world are you living in? Now, quit being a wimp and fix it."

"No way. I'm out. *You* fix it. Tonight."

THREE

Thunder rumbled, shaking the air surrounding the mourners who'd come to the afternoon funeral to say goodbye to Suzanne Miller. Thankfully, heavy rain continued to hold off, but Marianna knew it wouldn't hold much longer. The fine mist they'd started the service with had progressed to a steady drizzle; soon it would be a downpour. She clutched the curved handle of her umbrella and scanned the crowd.

She spotted Ethan and Catelyn a few yards away, looking alert and watching those gathered. Their diligent surveillance sent a shiver crawling up her spine to settle at the base of her neck.

The minister spoke but she couldn't see his face clearly through the sea of shifting heads and the service wasn't interpreted, so Marianna couldn't actually understand much of anything being said. Which gave her time to focus on the people.

She knew a lot of them, their sad faces grabbing her heart. But it was Suzanne's parents who speared her emotions and clogged her throat with tears yet again. Unmitigated grief, stunned disbelief and rampant rage alternated across their faces. Marianna could relate. She hoped they'd gotten everything they'd wanted from the house this morning. Suzanne hadn't had a lot of things and as soon as the police had cleared the scene, her family had wanted to gather the last of their loved one's items.

Marianna shivered again. When she took her focus off
Suzanne's family, became aware of her surroundings, she
felt…watched. After finally admitting the unsettling sensation wasn't just in her imagination, her stomach quivered.

And then she realized…he probably was here.

Suzanne's killer might be somewhere in this crowd.

She'd heard of killers showing up at their victims' funerals
but couldn't fathom that she might actually be standing somewhere near a murderer. Shuddering, she wrapped an arm
around her middle in a one-arm hug.

Fear churned; she swallowed it down.

Ever since the viewing and short service at the church, and
then upon arrival at the burial site, she'd felt someone staring
holes in her back. Yet each time she turned, she saw nothing
strange and no one out of place. At first, she chalked it up to
being the dead woman's roommate. Of course people would
stare at her.

But maybe it was more than that.

As though in slow motion, she turned a full circle, examining every face, trying to see around hats, scarves and umbrellas.

Movement caught from the corner of her eye brought her
head around. Ethan headed her way. Nerves cluttered up her
stomach. If he leaned over and whispered in her ear, would
she be able to catch the words? Pulling the collar of her coat
snug around her neck, she stepped to the left to get a better
view of the minister. She'd been invited to sit with the family,
but the number of relatives in attendance had clearly been
underestimated, so Marianna had surrendered her chair to an
elderly aunt.

Ethan stepped next to her. She looked up at him. He smiled
and mouthed, "Are you all right?"

She shrugged, ignored the threat of tears for the hundredth
time that day, then dared to ask, "He's here, isn't he?"

Ethan didn't bother to pretend he didn't understand who
she meant. She could see it in his eyes. "Probably." Keeping

his voice low, he looked over her shoulder and asked, "Do you see anyone who *shouldn't* be here?"

Once again, Marianna let her eyes trail over the people. The minister had finished and the mourners started their exit. "There're too many people, too many hats and umbrellas. I can't see all of their faces."

"I'm having that problem, too." His eyes scanned the group, but his body remained relaxed, hands tucked loosely in his pockets. "Who did you come with?"

"Just myself. My parents didn't know Suzanne very well, and my dad wasn't feeling well anyway, so Mom wouldn't let him come out in the cold." She paused, bit her lip and looked away from him. "I spent the night at my parents' house again last night. I just couldn't…I guess tonight I'll stay at my house." Tears pooled and this time she couldn't fight them. Several dribbled down her cold cheeks.

A warm cloth swept them away. Ethan had pulled out a handkerchief. Grateful, she took it from his hand and finished mopping up. "Thanks. I'm sorry. I suppose the tears will stop one day."

"Let yourself grieve. It's okay to hurt. And it's okay to stay with your parents awhile. No one would blame you." All gentleness and compassion, his eyes said he hurt for her.

She pocketed the handkerchief. "I'll wash it and get it back to you."

"No hurry. Come here." He took her hand in his and urged her along behind him.

She followed, stopping when he placed a hand on her arm. Wondering what he was doing, she watched his face, waiting for him to speak. "Okay, now, you can see the people getting in their cars. Tell me if you see anyone who sticks out."

Marianna turned. She and Ethan stood at the top of a gently sloping hill, making it easy to watch the crowd scatter to their various vehicles below. The rain had slacked off.

People closed their umbrellas, affording Marianna a pretty good view of faces she hadn't been able to see earlier.

She gasped, "There's Bryson."

"The ex-boyfriend, right?"

"Yes. I mean, I don't know why I'm surprised he's here. It was a mutual breakup without any hard feelings. Of course he would be here. I'm sure Suzanne's death came as a shock."

"I still want to talk to him and maybe catch him off guard so I'll see a true reaction. Excuse me, okay?"

Marianna watched the good-looking young attorney head for his black BMW. Ethan set off after the man, leaving her trailing slowly behind and watching the two of them. Then the feeling of being watched caused her to glance over her shoulder once more. Nothing and no one around her stood out as suspicious.

Her BlackBerry vibrated. Shoving her hand in her pocket, she kept her eyes on Ethan as he approached Bryson. When the device hummed again, she glanced at it. And groaned.

Curt Wentworth. Why wouldn't he leave her alone?

She flipped the cover and read his text.

"We need to talk. Stop being so stubborn and meet me this evening for dinner."

Not in this lifetime, buster. What would it take for him to get the message she wanted nothing more to do with him? He'd put his hands on her in anger and left bruises on her. He'd also been verbally abusive. He was the last person she wanted to have dinner with. For at least two minutes, she stared at it, debating what to say. Unable to come up with anything she wouldn't regret, she closed the unanswered message and the machine, clenching her fist around the device.

A gentle hand covered hers. Startled, she realized Ethan had come back. She shivered. And realized something else. The feel of his hand on hers felt right.

"Problem?" His brows climbed to reach into the shaggy blond hair that lay across on his forehead.

"What?" She'd missed what he'd said. Trying to speech read through a red fog of anger didn't come in her little bag of tricks.

"Is there a problem?" he repeated.

"Oh. Yes. But nothing I can't handle." And she would handle it. Just as soon as she figured out how.

"I don't mind helping out."

"I said I could handle it." She appreciated the offer but didn't need another person in her life trying to take care of her. Winning her independence had been a tough battle, but she'd done it.

Hands held up in a gesture of surrender, he backed up a little. "Gotcha."

Feeling a tad guilty at her snappiness when he'd been nothing short of wonderful, she bit her lip and sighed. "I'm sorry. I'm just a little…"

"…stressed," he finished for her. "Understandable."

"So, what did Bryson have to say?"

"I get the impression he was truly upset." Ethan recalled the man's red-rimmed eyes and genuine air of grief. "He said something about the fact that they'd been talking about getting back together."

"Really? I didn't know that."

"I asked him if he'd be willing to give us a DNA sample so the crime scene investigators could compare it with anything they found…if they find something. He said he'd go down first thing Monday morning."

"I always liked Bryson. I'm not exactly sure why they broke up, but I think he was pressuring Suzanne to get married and she wanted some space. She never really talked about it, though, even with me." She shrugged. "I didn't push, figuring she'd tell me if she wanted to."

Ethan watched her features, marveling once again at her physical beauty. And yet she was so much more than just a pretty package. In just the short time he'd known her and under the worst circumstances, she'd shown herself to be the epitome of...what? He searched his brain for the right adjective.

Class. The woman was pure class.

Shadowed dark brown eyes stared at him, and he realized he hadn't responded to something she'd said. "Sorry, my mind went wandering." No sense in telling her where.

Marianna flashed a dimpled smile, brief but sincere. "It's fine. I was just saying that I needed to get...home." She grimaced, and he knew she wasn't excited about the idea. After a minuscule hesitation, she took his hand between hers and gave it a quick squeeze, her closeness and light, fruity perfume scrambling his senses. Biting her lip, she gave him a shaky smile. "Thank you for everything. I hope you'll keep me updated on the case."

"Absolutely."

Marianna left the cemetery and began the short drive home. She dreaded going into her house alone, yet had turned down several offers of accompaniment. Not exactly sure why, she just knew she didn't want to be around a bunch of people, including family. She knew she faced a lot of cleaning up and most likely more uncontrollable tears. Better to do that without an audience. Ethan had started to insist that he follow her but had gotten a call and had to leave. That had been fine with her.

She'd texted Joseph, asking him to bring Twister home so the dog would be there to greet her. He'd agreed against his better judgment, arguing she didn't need to be by herself.

She pulled into the driveway and turned the car off. The house loomed, small and empty. It shouldn't seem particularly scary, yet a tremor shook her at the thought of walking up the path to her porch. Memories almost overwhelmed her, tempting her to once again run home to her mom and dad.

At least the door was closed today. Please, God, take this

fear away. I know it's only natural after what's happened, but I don't want to be afraid. Help me trust You.

The curtain in the window to the right of the door moved; a black nose pressed against the glass. The familiar sight caused her to release a relieved breath.

Twister's welcome home. He was waiting for her.

Marianna scrambled from the car, grabbing the overnight bag Joseph had packed for her the day of the murder, and headed for the door.

Climbing the steps, she paused, noticing the footprint had disappeared. Someone had scrubbed it away. Shuddering, unease still very much present, she unlocked the door and pushed it open.

And gaped.

Her house sparkled, from top to bottom. Someone had scrubbed, mopped, vacuumed and more.

How…what…who?

Ethan.

She frowned. Now why did she automatically assume it was him? It could have been Joseph or some other member of her family.

Someone had hired a professional to clean up the mess left by the criminal and the crime scene investigators. Her heart warmed at the thoughtfulness as grateful tears blurred her vision. A piece of paper lay on the table just inside the foyer. Picking it up, she read, "I didn't want you to come home to a mess. Hope everything is better than when you left it. Ethan."

"Thank you, Ethan," she whispered.

Twister nudged her hand and whined. Absentmindedly, she scratched his head as she went from room to room, examining everything.

A lump clogged her throat as she moved, sensing Suzanne's presence even though she was now with the Lord.

When she reached Suzanne's room, the door stood open, inviting. Hitching her breath, she stepped in and looked around. It, too, had been scrupulously cleaned.

And stripped bare. Suzanne's family had come and gone, leaving not even a trace of their presence. Or Suzanne's. Unable to stop herself, she looked to the spot where her roommate had died.

Even the stain was gone. It was as if Suzanne had never been there. Marianna walked over and knelt, running her hand over the area, feeling the carpet spring back beneath her palm. Anger, fear and a troubled helplessness burned within her.

Help the police find her killer. And help me deal with this, Lord. Please give me peace.

Tired beyond belief, Marianna called to Twister and stepped from the room, pulling the door shut behind her.

Entering her bedroom next door, she stared at the familiar sight of her haven that was supposed to offer comfort and knew she couldn't sleep here tonight. Her stomach rumbled, but she had no energy to fix anything to eat. Doing a one-eighty, she trod the short distance to the small living area and crashed on the couch. She pulled out her hearing aids and laid them on the end table beside her.

All sound ceased to exist for her, and all she wanted to do was snuggle into the silence.

Twister settled on the floor beside her and she let her hand dangle over the edge to rest on his back as she stared at the ceiling, thinking, praying, drifting....

With a start, Marianna's eyes popped open, confusion holding her captive until her brain caught up. She'd fallen asleep on the couch. But something had awakened her. A vibration: Twister?

Darkness blanketed the room broken only by the glow of the night-light coming from the hall. The clock on the DVD player read 3:18 a.m.

What had awakened her? Rubbing her face, then running a hand through her tangled hair, she swung her feet to the floor, eyes probing the blackness. That was odd. Where was Twister?

Uneasiness swept over her. The hardwoods floor beneath

her trembled. No doubt the vibrations had awakened her. Fingers groped the table beside her, grabbed up her hearing aids and shoved them in her ears.

Still, mostly silence surrounded her.

Again the floor shook. As though cushioning a footstep? Uneasiness climbed into fear. She strained to hear something, anything. Her breathing quickened as spider feet scrabbled up her spine. Her stomach cramped with a sudden thought, what if the killer had come back?

Would he do that? But why?

Adrenaline pumping, she fumbled to remember where she'd left her purse, which held her BlackBerry.

The recliner. In the corner by the fireplace. Guided by eyes adjusting to the darkness and the dim hall light, she crept across the floor to the chair and shoved her hand into her purse, located the device and snatched it out.

She realized she still had her shoes on: low-heeled black pumps she'd worn to the funeral. Sliding them off, she set them aside and tried to think of a possible hiding place. The kitchen pantry? Or should she try to slip out the front door?

Lord, what do I do?

A sense of urgency caused her hands to shake. She felt more vibrations and a hard thud sent her adrenaline into overdrive. Was that a muttered curse she picked up? She inched the volume up on her hearing aid but had to be careful not to bump it up too far or it would start whistling.

Then she tuned in to Twister's furious barking, causing her to flinch. He'd probably been barking for a while if he'd already reached the pitch she needed to hear him.

With her heart thudding and her blood pounding, her brain switched to survival mode. Her fingers found the numbers on her BlackBerry and punched Send.

She needed help fast.

Someone was in her house.

FOUR

Ethan leaned back in the squeaky chair, tapping the pencil against his chin, staring at the ceiling as weariness washed over him. He should be in bed. But the nightmare had returned full force, and his escape to his desk had been the only thing that had allowed him to push the memories to the back of his mind.

Thankfully, it hadn't been the dream about the death of his sister. Unfortunately, it had been the one about his other failure. A hostage situation. The one where he'd been in charge and the woman had died. He'd just finished his crisis negotiation training, fresh from his sister's funeral...and drunk. Oh, not stumbling, falling-down drunk, but he'd definitely had one too many. And he'd made a very bad decision that cost a young woman her life. At least he felt as if it was his fault. He was supposed to have had backup, someone with more experience, but the man hadn't shown up in time. So, it had fallen to Ethan...and he'd failed.

His fault...all his fault.

The words echoed in his mind. *I'm sorry, God. Are You listening? I'm sorry.*

The pencil snapped with a crack. Startled, Ethan dropped the pieces to his desk, then rubbed his bleary eyes, wishing he could make it all go away. But he couldn't.

So, here he sat at approximately three o'clock in the morning, trying to make sense of Suzanne's murder. The place wasn't exactly a ghost town, since other officers, suffering a similar affliction to Ethan's, chose to work the graveyard shift. He grimaced when realizing he felt more comfortable at his desk than he did in his home.

His personal cell vibrated on his hip, and he sat up with a start. Who in the world...? A quick glance at the caller ID showed Marianna's cell number. He'd memorized it with ease the first time he'd seen it in her file.

Dread hit his chest. She must be in trouble. Why else would she be calling at this time of night...morning. With his left hand, he grabbed his keys; with his right, he pulled the phone from the clip.

"Hello?"

No answer.

"Hello?" He raced for the door and down to his car. She couldn't hear him, but surely she could see that he'd answered. Why didn't she say something?

Unless she couldn't. He had the bad feeling his first reaction—that she was in trouble—was right. Indecision, fear of making the wrong move, made him pause for a fraction of a second; then he found himself praying. A simple litany. Let me get there in time. Let me save her.

Bolting from the office, he raced for his car.

Marianna prayed silently as she felt another tremor beneath her stockinged feet. The vibration felt stronger. Once again she had called 911 and had no way of knowing if the police were on the way. She'd placed a call to Ethan as backup, praying he would wake up to hear his phone ringing.

More vibrations. Was that a door slamming? It felt closer. Was he searching for her? Whatever he was doing, he was heading her way. Panting her fear, she clung desperately to control, forcing her mind to think, to reason, to figure a way out. Visions of Suzanne lying on her bedroom floor, blood pooling beneath her head, caused a wave of nausea followed by dizziness to rush through her.

Her world turned choppy, the survival instinct strong. Her eyes darted around the room.

The fireplace. The poker. A weapon.

Then a thump. Vibrations. Marianna quickly moved toward the front door, her hand now on the knob. It was locked, of course.

More of Twister's furious barking, then nothing. Worry for her pet churned within her. Oh, God, protect Twister. Did she have time to get out, or should she hide? Would whoever was in her house come looking for her? How much time had the dog bought her?

Shaking hands fumbled with the dead bolt. Precious seconds ticked by as the key fell to the floor. The thumping stopped, vibrations ceased. She froze, her breath strangling her as she tried not to gasp, desperately wishing she could hear how much noise she was making.

Her BlackBerry buzzed in her pocket; she ignored it. Trembling, she bent down, snatched the key, jammed it in the lock and finally got the door open. She slipped out the opening, onto the porch, and felt hard hands grasp her upper arms.

Marianna's screech nearly ruptured Ethan's eardrums. He hadn't meant to scare her, but she'd come stumbling out the door so fast that if he hadn't caught her, she'd have taken them both to the floor of the cement porch.

Twisting, struggling against him, she had her eyes closed. "Marianna, it's me." *She can't understand with her eyes closed, remember?*

Not knowing whether to let go or give her a shake, he figured releasing her might surprise her into opening her eyes. He let go and stepped back. She stumbled, gasped and opened terror-filled, tar-black eyes to stare at him. Finally, recognition dawned, and relief swept away the fear...for a moment. Then she whispered, "He's in my house. I dialed 911, so the police should be on the way."

Ethan set her behind him and stepped in. His right hand pulled his ever-present gun from his shoulder holster. Pointing the weapon to the ceiling, he turned and mouthed to Marianna, "Stay here, okay?"

She nodded, then whispered in a small, worried voice, "Something's happened to Twister, too. He was barking his head off, then stopped abruptly. So be careful."

Lips tight, Ethan gave a nod, pulled his cell phone from the clip on his belt and dialed a number requesting backup. After he hung up, he stepped back farther into the house. He started to shut the door—only to stop when Marianna stepped in behind him. He frowned at her. "I told you to stay out here."

"Please, I'll stand right here." Fear oozed from her, and his heart clenched in anger at the person doing this to her.

A small crash from the back of the house snapped his attention in that direction. If the noise was coming from back there, she was probably fine standing next to the door—probably. He gave her another pointed look, then started making his way toward the sound, nerves tense, senses alert.

A whispered curse followed by the sound of glass breaking.

Then silence once again.

With quick, measured steps, he headed toward the back room, gun ready. Adrenaline flowed, but he kept his breathing steady. The memory of the first time he'd entered the house haunted him. He felt as if he was in a time warp, déjà-vu kind of thing. Ignoring the sensation, he moved into the first bedroom on his left.

Marianna's room. Empty. Except for shards of broken glass littering the area under her window and—his gut clenched—Twister, lying motionless at the foot of the bed.

Marianna cowered by the front door, torn with the desire to run and the determination to back up Ethan should he need it. Squaring her shoulders, she watched Ethan disappear down the hall, then crept over to the fireplace to grab the poker she'd considered earlier.

Hefting the weight of it in her right hand, she felt slightly more prepared to face the danger that lay just down the hall. *Oh Lord, protect Ethan. And I know Twister's just a dog, but please take care of him.*

The hardwood floor vibrated once more, and she tightened her grip on the makeshift weapon, ready to swing if an unfamiliar face appeared in front of her.

But it was only Ethan, looking grim and tight-lipped. He held up a finger as he walked past her to the front door and yanked it open. Flashing red-and-blue lights fought for space in the small opening. The cops were here, she realized belatedly.

Her gaze followed Ethan's retreating back as he flashed his badge to the two startled officers, who'd started grabbing at their guns the minute the door opened. At the sight of the badge and the man behind it, they relaxed. He said something and their posture tensed once again. One took off around the side of the house; Ethan went the other way, and the third man walked toward Marianna.

She looked at him. "What's going on?"

"I'm Officer Tom Bell. Ethan thinks the guy slipped out of your bedroom window and headed off through those woods in the back. Ethan didn't want to follow him out the window in case the guy left behind some evidence." He kept his face turned toward her and enunciated his words clearly. Ethan must have told him she couldn't hear. She didn't know whether to be annoyed or appreciative. She settled for appreciation...this time.

Within minutes the two men were back. The disgust on Ethan's features said whoever had been in her house had escaped.

Dread crept around in her stomach, finally settling in a hard knot at the pit. She looked at Ethan. "Now what?"

"We need to get the crime scene team back over here and

see if he left any evidence behind." Concern slid across his face as he laid a hand on her shoulder. "Twister's hurt. Who's your vet?"

"Oh, no." She whirled to rush back into the house. His hand grasped her upper arm, halting her progress. She spun around. "What?"

"Let me get him. I don't want you destroying any evidence."

"Is it bad?" Anguish squeezed her heart.

"I don't think so. The guy hit him with the lamp from your end—" Ethan blinked, his attention caught by something behind her. She followed his gaze—Twister slowly made his way down the hall, his eyes cloudy with pain but fixed on his mistress. A trickle of blood made its way from the middle of his head down over his brown-and-black snout.

"Oh, Twister," she whispered, dropping to her knees. He came slowly, weaving slightly. When he arrived at Marianna, he dropped to the floor with a cross between a whimper and a grunt to lay his head on her knee.

"Will you make the call for me?" She wondered if he could hear the tears she felt clogging her throat as she asked him the favor.

"Sure." He squeezed her hand in silent sympathy and pulled his phone from the clip. She looked up the number on her BlackBerry and Ethan complied.

As once again her house flooded with authorities and crime scene investigators, Marianna gave her statement, then sat in the back of Ethan's car, hugging her beloved pet to her as Ethan drove them to the vet's office.

After leaving Marianna's dog at the emergency veterinarian's office, Ethan replayed his part in the scene of the break-in. What had he done wrong? How had he let the guy get away?

Fatigue gripped him. It had been a long while since he'd had a good night's sleep. And now the sun crept toward the horizon. Soon it would be dawn…and he'd yet to go to bed. Oh well, he'd survive.

Marianna, however…"Hey," he said as he touched her arm. She swung her head around to look at him. He kept his face angled toward her so she could see his lips but he was still able to keep his eyes safely on the road. "Where do you want to go, your parents'?"

She gave a listless shrug. "I guess so."

"Twister is going to be all right. You heard the doctor."

Marianna blew out a sigh. "I know and I'm grateful, but I'm also terribly frustrated. What is going on, Ethan?" Tears surfaced once again. He watched as she held them at bay with sheer determination.

He shook his head. "I don't know, Marianna. I think you're the only one who can really answer that. Unfortunately, you might not even know what you know."

"Well, that's clear."

A rueful chuckle slipped out. "I'm sorry. I wish had something more to tell you."

"I've racked my brain trying to come up with something. Why someone would kill Suzanne? Why did, possibly, the same someone come back to the house and was willing to break in with me there?" She turned thoughtful. "Although, he may not have known anyone was there, because I parked my car in the garage when I got home." Her eyes narrowed. "Do you think he's looking for something?"

Ethan pulled into her parents' driveway and glanced at the dashboard clock. It read 6:42. "It's certainly a possibility. At first, when I got to your house the day of the murder, I thought there'd been a huge fight in Suzanne's room. But there was no evidence she'd struggled. So, it could be the guy was definitely looking for something. Could Suzanne have been involved in something shady? Something you wouldn't have known about?"

"Absolutely not." She spoke without hesitation. "Suze

was a great girl and a devoted Christian. There's no way she would be associated with something illegal."

"Then the incidents may not be related. It's possible our burglar read the story about Suzanne's murder in the paper, did a simple online search to find out where Suzanne lived and decided to help himself to anything he could find."

"Only I was there." She frowned, her dark, finely arched brows coming together above the bridge of her delicate nose. "It mentioned me in the article, so he had to know she had a roommate."

"Maybe. Then again, he may have figured no roommate would want to stay in a house all by herself after her friend had been killed in said house, and therefore he would have free reign."

She rolled her eyes, her gorgeous, chocolate eyes. He blinked. She was saying, "There are so many possible explanations it makes my head hurt. Thank you for having my house cleaned up, by the way. That was a very thoughtful thing to do."

Ethan could feel the heat rising to his face. He didn't really know why he was embarrassed; it was just that her smile did crazy things to his emotions. He reached out to brush a finger under her hair, to push it away from her face, then moved his hand, cupping her cheek. "You're quite welcome." She looked...kissable. He leaned closer and let his hand slide to the back of her neck.

The porch light came on; a face appeared in the window. Ethan felt another flush start to creep up his neck as he slowly pulled back, turning from the watchful eyes peering at them from behind the glass and connecting his gaze with Marianna's once more. He felt as if he was back in high school on a date and his girl's dad had just sent him a warning.

Marianna's short, lilting laugh told him she'd read his thoughts. He smiled at her. "Aw, stop," he drawled. She grinned, her dimples flashed and his heart sputtered. Crazy.

A light tap on his window jerked his attention from the woman beside him. He pressed the button and the glass slid down in a smooth ride. A tall, dark-haired, dark-eyed male replica of Marianna stared down at him. In his early thirties, the man had the air of one who knew what he wanted and had what it took to get it.

Ethan had the uneasy feeling this man wanted him, or at least Marianna, out of the car.

Marianna leaned forward and asked, "Joseph, what are you doing up?"

"When I hear a car pull up in the driveway and then silence, I'm going to investigate a bit." Sarcasm dripped, but Ethan could tell the man wasn't angry. Joseph, FBI agent and big brother. He could handle the FBI agent part; it was the big brother part that had him leery. But there was no way he was letting that little secret become public knowledge. Ethan gave Joseph a cool nod and held eye contact as he shoved open his door.

Joseph stepped back and Marianna took the cue to climb out her side. She walked around and slid her arms around Joseph's waist. Ethan felt a twinge of jealousy that took him by surprise as her brother gave her a comforting hug. He wished she trusted him that way. Then he gave a mental roll of his eyes and told himself to get it together.

He said, "Marianna had another little incident early this morning."

Joseph's gaze sharpened. "What kind of incident?"

"Someone broke in my house. Twister scared him off. I called 911 but must have hung up too soon. I couldn't tell if someone answered or not. Then I called Ethan and he came to the rescue. Now, I want to go to bed."

Joseph's expression said he wouldn't be satisfied with that piddling explanation, but wasn't going to push it for now because he could see the exhaustion on her face. Ethan's respect for the man went up a notch...and it was already high to begin with.

The light flickered off, then on, then off, then back on—a way of getting a deaf person's attention. Marianna pulled away from Joseph, turned and saw her mother standing on the porch, her fingers on the light switch. The glow from the ceiling fan light illuminated the area. She signed. "Hey, Mom, it's just me. I'm moving back in for a little while, if that's okay."

Questions formed in her mother's eyes, but she didn't say anything, just motioned for Marianna to come in. Then she gave a pointed look at Ethan. Marianna signed, "Mom, meet Ethan O'Hara. He's the detective working on Suzanne's case." Then she said, "Ethan, meet my mother, Maddelena Santino."

Ethan walked toward the women, his smile sincere and charming at the same time. He signed, "Nice to meet you." Surprise lit Maddelena's eyes and Marianna gasped.

He directed a sad smile toward her as he signed and spoke at the same time. "Yes, I sign. I had a deaf sister. She was...she died...three years ago, but I've never forgotten her language."

Marianna thought her jaw might hit the ground. Then her mother said with graceful hands, "It's freezing out here. Everyone come in and let me feed you breakfast."

Her mother's answer to every disaster: Food. Right now, Marianna wouldn't complain. With her life so crazy, she'd welcome the familiar routine. Plus, she was cold and wanted to get inside.

Once Maddelena had everyone settled, she fired up the gas stove and cooked a breakfast fit for a five-star restaurant. The rest of her family made their way into the kitchen, and the introductions began.

Her terror fading in the chaos of family, Marianna felt herself relaxing and enjoying Ethan's shell-shocked look. She said, "You don't come from a large family, do you?"

He shook his head. "Nope. It was just me for a long time.

My sister was almost ten years younger. Then, she died...."
He trailed off, his gaze fixed on two of her siblings arguing over who got the next piece of toast. Alonso, her sixteen-year-old deaf brother and youngest member of the clan, had lightning-fast reflexes and beat out Gina, her twenty-six-year-old hearing sister who was a real estate attorney in North Carolina. Gina had come home last week to visit and announce her recent engagement.

Gina punched Alonso in the arm hard enough to make him wince. She signed, "You need to learn to respect your elders, boy."

Alonso signed back, "When I see an elder that deserves it, I'll give it."

Gina very maturely stuck out her tongue, then turned her back on him to plop another piece of bread in the toaster.

Marianna smiled at the craziness. She told Ethan, "If you think this is bad, you should see us all at Christmas!"

"I can't even imagine." He took a bite of his eggs and chewed, but she noticed he never took his eyes from the antics of her family.

She also noticed Alonso refused to look in Ethan's direction. Lasering the evil eye on her brother, she subtly signed, "He's not the cop who arrested you. Be nice." Unfortunately, about six months ago, Alonso had been arrested for being in the wrong place at the wrong time when a friend of his decided to shoplift. Protesting his innocence to this day, he still had an aversion to cops. Including his own brother, Joseph.

Alonso rolled his eyes and ignored her order.

Then she noticed Ethan's frown. He placed his fork on his plate and reached for his phone, lifting it to his ear. He listened for a minute and a half, then hung up. His fierce expression was back, his tenseness from the break-in returning twofold.

She raised a brow in question.

He signed, "That was Catelyn. The lab found some

evidence, and I need to get over there to find out what's going on."

"On a Saturday?"

He gave a small smile. "No rest for the weary." When he stood, everyone looked up at him. He signed, "It was a pleasure to meet you all, but duty calls."

Marianna's mother frowned and signed back, "They don't let you eat?"

Joseph shot him a sympathetic glance and saved him from having to answer by saying, "Mama, you know how it is in law enforcement. You've got to do what you can when you can."

Maddelena rolled her dark eyes and signed, "Bah, you go do your job, then, but only if you promise to come back when you can eat a decent meal. And come to church with us tomorrow. We go to the church with the interpreter on the other side of town."

Ethan said his thanks for the breakfast, made no comment about church and headed out the door.

Marianna stabbed a bite of pancake as she watched him leave, wondering why the fact that he was so comfortable with her family made her nervous.

Ethan climbed into his car, never so glad to get out of someone's home. Not that he hadn't enjoyed the crazy clan, but they made him think about the past. About what might have been.

Guilt pierced him as it did every time he thought about his sister, Ashley. And the more he was around Marianna, the more he thought about Ashley. A vicious cycle if there ever was one.

Poor Ashley. She'd been ten years his junior and stuck with him as the one person she could count on...and he'd let her down. True, it hadn't been intentional, but in the end it hadn't mattered. She'd died.

And his life had spiraled downward into a hole he'd almost

been unable to claw his way out of. If it hadn't been for his ex-partner, Mac McCullough, Ethan might still be drowning his sorrows in a six-pack each night. Mac had eventually quit the force and gone on to be a missionary overseas, but Ethan thanked God for the man every day.

His phone rang, yanking him from his memories. Thank goodness. "Hello."

"Hey, it's Catelyn. Where are you?"

"Almost to the lab. Why?"

"We got a shoe print from under her window."

"Does it match the bloody one from the porch?"

"Nope. Unfortunately, not."

"Are they the same size?"

"Negative on that, too."

"All that means is that the guy wore a different pair of shoes."

"Or this break-in is totally unrelated to the murder." Ethan could hear her frustration. She wanted to catch this guy as bad as he did.

He said, "Yeah, I've already thought of that."

"So, what's Marianna going to do? Is she staying with her folks right now? I'm really nervous about her going back to that house by herself. Something's just weird about the whole situation. The murder, then the break-in…weird."

"I agree. But I'm stumped as to a connection. And yes, right now, she's staying with her folks." He sighed, ran a hand through his already mussed hair. "Listen, I haven't been to bed yet. If you don't actually need me there, I'm going to run home, take a shower and crash for a couple of hours."

"Sure, I've got it covered. Go get some rest and call me when you get up. I appreciate you not calling me in on it last night."

"Nothing much you could have done. I didn't figure you'd hate me for letting you sleep."

"Never. That's why I'm willing to put in a few hours on the weekend. I'll get it back after we catch this guy."

"Thanks, Cate."

He hung up, did a U-turn, then took a left to head home. Just a few hours sleep, then he'd be back on it, he silently promised himself...and Marianna.

FIVE

As Marianna dressed for church in the morning, she studied the childhood room she'd shared with two of her sisters, Catherina and Alissa. She smiled when she thought of her twin, Alissa.

As children and even teens, they hadn't wanted to be separated and had shared a room up until graduation from high school. They'd gone to different colleges, Marianna to Gallaudet University in Washington, D.C. and Alissa to the University of South Carolina in Columbia, just a couple of hours away.

Being the parents of six children, her mother and father had had to get creative when it came to sleeping arrangements. The house had four bedrooms and a basement that had been converted into a small apartment for Marianna's grandmother, who'd lived with them until she died last year.

Marianna appreciated the fact that her mother still kept the double bed and bunk beds in here so that the sisters could have their "reunion" during holidays. Often all four sisters usually wound up in the one room, staying up all night catching up, then crashing wherever they found a spot.

She said a small prayer of thanks for her childhood, knowing she'd been blessed. Oh, not always with material things but with the things that mattered. And one more thing to be thankful for was the fact that the vet had sent a text message saying Twister would be able to come home Monday. Marianna missed her four-legged friend.

Attached to the pocket of her black dress pants, her Black-Berry buzzed, pulling her from her thoughts. She slipped it from the clip and checked the caller ID.

Curt Wentworth. Why he continued to bother her, she had yet to figure out. This was the man who'd wooed her, had her tumbling head over heels in love, then had turned around and emotionally stabbed her in the back. When he finally let her know she wasn't good enough for him. Add his physical aggression into the mix and she just wanted him to leave her alone. She read, "Why aren't you answering my messages? I want to see you, Marianna. It really makes me mad when you just ignore me. Rather rude, don't you think? At least have the courtesy to answer me."

She punched the reply button on the machine and typed, "Leave me alone, please, Curt. ALREADY TOLD YOU I'M NOT INTERESTED IN SEEING YOU ANYMORE. If you would stop texting me, I wouldn't have to ignore you. You are the one being rude."

He responded, "But I've apologized, what else can I do?"

"Honor my request to LEAVE ME ALONE."

"I made a mistake, Marianna. As a Christian, aren't you supposed to forgive me?"

This called for caps again. "I HAVE FORGIVEN YOU, JUST DON'T WANT TO BE WITH YOU. I wouldn't mind trying to build a friendship with you, but it would go no further than that, and you and I both know that you're unwilling to accept that right now. Late for church. Bye."

She replaced the device back into the clip and grabbed her purse. When it vibrated once more, she pressed the 'Ignore' button, resolving not to respond to him anymore. Maybe that was the problem. She kept answering him intermittently instead of being consistent in just deleting his messages, and that encouraged him or gave him hope. Quite possibly if she just didn't acknowledge his texts anymore, he would give up and go find someone more suitable.

Such as a hearing girl, one he wouldn't be ashamed of. Absentmindedly, she smoothed her hair down over her ears, then stared at herself in the mirror above the dresser. In a fit of pique, she grabbed a hair tie and pulled the silky mass into a casual ponytail, exposing her hearing aids for the world to see. There. Eat your heart out, Curt Wentworth.

Marianna clamped the lid on the memories and the feelings they still invoked. Not feelings for him, just the feelings of not measuring up or being good enough.

He'd certainly fooled her for a long time. But she'd learned her lesson well. And while she'd been honest when she'd said she'd forgiven him, she sure hadn't forgotten his behavior. Or his constant pushing for her to get a cochlear implant, a surgically implanted device that worked as a "mechanical ear." It was great for some people, she just chose not to go that route right now. She shook her head at her stupidity. He could have asked her for almost anything that wasn't illegal or immoral, and she would have done her best to oblige.

Anything but to get a cochlear implant. And he'd refused to listen to her or her reasons why she didn't want one. She didn't want to risk destroying the hearing she had left. She was also comfortable with her deafness and didn't need to be "fixed." It was a concept Curt couldn't compute and refused to accept that she knew her own mind on this topic. Marianna grimaced. *Okay, Lord, give me something more pleasant to think about this morning, please?*

Immediately, Ethan's face appeared in her mind's eye. She grabbed her jacket as she allowed herself to think about the good-looking cop. She'd been surprised he'd fit in so well with her family—and to find out he'd had a deaf sister...well...

The lamp on her bedside table flashed. All of the bedrooms were wired with a flashing light to alert the occupant that someone was "knocking" on the door. There was actually a small button to push, similar to an indoor doorbell that activated the light.

She opened her door to find Gina standing on the other side. Her sister signed, "You ready?"

"Yes, I guess. Curt's bugging me again this morning."

Her sister sighed and shook her head. "I hope you told him to leave you alone."

They started the walk down the hall to the stairs. Gina turned and walked backward down the steps, gripping the rail with her left hand as she signed with her right. Marianna smiled at the leftover childhood behavior and answered, "I did, but it doesn't seem to faze him much."

Gina, dark hair, dark eyes and slightly overweight, still had all the features of the Santinos. Full lips and slightly slanted eyes gave her an exotic look, showing off her Italian heritage, but somewhere down the line the family had some Japanese blood, too. Her sister wore it well.

"Want me to get rid of him for you? I know a guy or two."

"No, I wouldn't want to get Mario in trouble before you guys even get married." Her sister's fiancé was an army ranger. "I'll handle Curt. Now, let's get to church."

The rest of the family, including her father, who was finally looking a little better after his bout with whatever had laid him low the last couple of weeks, dispersed to their respective cars. Marianna rode with Gina, who planned to have lunch with friends after church. As they drove, Marianna couldn't help thinking about the break-in from Friday night. As much as she didn't want to, she remembered the terror she'd felt, the pure fear that had almost held her paralyzed.

Did the guy find what he was after? Did that incident have anything to do with Suzanne's murder?

She shivered in spite of the heat blowing from the vents.

Would he be back? Would she feel safe staying there by herself now, unable to hear if danger came prowling again?

A nagging sense of unease kept her nerves on edge. She couldn't seem to focus on anything much but the continued flashes of remembered terror.

Think of something else!

Her parents and Alonso led the way ahead of them. Marianna looked in the side mirror to watch the traffic behind them, mulling over her options: Stay in a house where she'd constantly be scared. Go stay with her parents. Move in with a friend from school.

None of the options really appealed to her. As she'd told her mother, it looked as if she would be moving back home temporarily.

A silver sedan with tinted windows cruised sedately behind her and Gina. At the traffic light, the man in the green SUV that pulled up next to her seemed to be watching her. She smiled, then kept her eyes straight ahead. The SUV turned right and she wilted. *Paranoia is only a good thing when someone's after you,* she reminded herself. *Otherwise they lock you up in the loony bin, okay? Relax.*

By the time they reached the church, Marianna's nerves were shot. And it didn't help that the silver sedan that had been following them most of the way turned into the parking lot behind her.

Feeling refreshed from a good night's sleep, yet antsy at the lack of progress in the case, Ethan determined to work on finding the man—or men—who'd broken into Marianna's home. He needed to see her, to dig deeper into her past and Suzanne's.

You've already done that, O'Hara. You're just looking for an excuse to see her.

The thought taunted him. He blew out a sigh. Oh, all right, he admitted it. He wanted to see her. But he really did need to hash the case out with her, too. Sometimes the victim is so busy being the victim that he or she subconsciously refuses to bring memories to the surface until later, after the passage of time when once again the individual is feeling secure, safe.

Acting completely out of character, Ethan impulsively decided to meet her when she came out of church and see if she would have lunch with him. He'd almost gotten up to go, but had wimped out at the last minute. It had been a while since he'd been to the large church downtown that his parents had frequented. Since Ashley's death, it just hurt to go back and be reminded of how much she'd loved being a part of the youth ministry, how much she'd loved giving to and serving others. But maybe he'd been wrong. Maybe if he'd have let people reach out to him…

Questioning his motives during the ten-minute drive to the church she'd mentioned attending, the one with a small deaf ministry, he pulled up outside of the sanctuary to sit and stare at the door. After a few minutes, his gaze wandered and the political poster in the window of the building across the street caught his attention.

It was election year and the campaigning was fast and furious, narrowing the candidates down one by one. Clayton Robertson seemed to be the favored one of the more conservative party, while Terrance Sloane ran a strong opposition.

Should be an interesting political year all the way up to the day in November when people would stand in line and vote in the next governor of South Carolina.

Ethan shook his head. He was all for democracy, but the money that went into these campaigns galled him. When he thought of the good those funds could do and how he always wondered if was spent as it was supposed to be, he shook his head and sighed. Well, he voted; not much else he could do about politicians and their issues.

A movement from the doorway of the church pulled him back to the reason he was here.

Marianna Santino.

A whole herd of people stampeded toward their vehicles after shaking hands with the pastor standing at the sanctuary exit. Finally, Marianna came out signing animatedly with a young girl. Ethan didn't mean to eavesdrop, but he caught that Marianna was reminding the girl about basketball practice tomorrow afternoon. The girl agreed, then said something about being ready for the big game on Thursday.

Ethan opened his door and stepped out, intending to approach Marianna and ask her to lunch, but he stopped when a clean-cut man in his early thirties walked up to her and took her hand. Regret cut through him. Who was this? A boyfriend?

Relief followed the regret when he saw her expression change to one of annoyance as she yanked her hand away from the guy.

Unfortunately, Ethan was too far away to hear what she was saying. But when the man grabbed her upper arm and Marianna winced, that was enough for him.

Marianna thought about giving Curt a good kick in the shin but didn't want to make a scene in the church parking lot. If he didn't let go of her arm in the next two seconds, however, she'd toss aside her inhibitions and give her foot permission to do its worst.

Then she was free, her arm throbbing from the grip Curt had had on it. What? How?

"Ethan? What are you doing here?" The question came out before she could stop it. Surprise and relief held her captive.

Fury emanated from his blue eyes and if he lasered Curt any harder with them, the poor man would be incinerated on the spot. Through gritted teeth, Ethan said, "Touch her again and I'll arrest you for assault."

Curt's Adam's apple bobbed. Then he bravely stuck out his chest. Funny how it seemed thin and pitiful next to Ethan's broad shoulders and muscular physique. Not that she had any business noticing that.

"Who are you?" Curt demanded.

Marianna stepped in. "This is Ethan, one of the detectives investigating Suzanne's death."

"Yeah," Ethan growled, "so where were you a week and a half ago on Tuesday, around ten in the morning?"

Curt's eyes shot wide and he stammered, "Um…uh…I… was at a conference…in…in New York."

Marianna elbowed her protector. "All right, Ethan, that's enough. Curt didn't kill Suzanne."

"What about breaking into your house?"

Curt looked ready for the ground beneath his feet to swallow him. "Look, I didn't kill anyone, and I certainly didn't break into Marianna's house. I don't have any reason to."

Marianna took Ethan's arm. "Come on. Walk with me to my mother's car. She's probably waiting on me."

Ethan gave a final, hard look at Curt and said, "My pleasure."

"Goodbye, Curt."

Marianna and Ethan headed in the direction she led. He asked, "Why'd you tell him bye?"

She blew out an exasperated breath. "I don't know. Because it was the polite thing to do?"

"When a man lays a hand on you like he did, the last thing he deserves is politeness. How's your arm?"

It hurt. "It's fine. Forget him and tell me why you're here."

Ethan spotted her parents and brother standing beside a white Suburban. "Why don't you have lunch with me and tell your folks I'll bring you home later?"

Nerves suddenly swirled in her stomach. What kind of lunch was he talking about? A date lunch? Or a business, let's-talk-about-the-case lunch? She bit her lip and he gave her a knowing smile.

"Please?"

She couldn't resist. "Okay." Catching her father's attention, she signed that she was going with Ethan and would be home later. He frowned but nodded.

Ethan took her hand and led her to his car.

That's when she noticed the silver car parked four spots down. Earlier, when it had turned in behind her and her sister, she'd tried to get a look at the driver, but it had gone on past them and around the side of the building. She'd given up trying to figure out if someone was following her and if the occupants of the car had been members of the church arriving at the same time as she.

Seeing the car still parked there, and her sister long gone, along with her parents, she decided she was definitely being paranoid—not that she didn't have good reason to be, but obviously the silver car belonged to a member of the congregation. Relief replaced her momentary anxiety.

Ethan tapped her shoulder to get her attention. "So, what are you in the mood for?" His touch lingered, causing her stomach to do a series of flip-flops.

Pushing her attraction aside for now, she thought. "Something...relaxing."

"Huh?"

"You know, relaxing food. Fruit, ice cream, soup."

"I never knew food could be relaxing."

Marianna reached up and took his hand in hers, feeling the calluses of a man used to hard work, yet one who used his hands for gentle comport, too. Somehow, Marianna knew Ethan would never raise a fist against her—ever.

"Well, you're about to learn something new. How about we go to Panera?"

"The one on East Main?"

She laughed. "Yes, since it's the only one in Spartanburg."

"Right." He pulled his hand from her grasp and cranked the car to head across town. Once there, Ethan ordered while she got a table. From her seat, she watched him smile at the young girl who flirted outrageously with him while punching in the order.

Marianna was impressed that while Ethan smiled in a friendly way, there was nothing encouraging or flirtatious about him. Curt would have...nope, not going there.

Soon, Ethan brought their food to the table, and Marianna enjoyed her salad while he sampled the soup.

After a few minutes, Marianna placed her fork on the table and looked at her companion. "So, let's get to the point. You have something else you want to discuss with me, don't you?"

Startled bemusement flickered briefly, then, turning serious, he said, "I don't think you're safe staying at your house."

"I've already thought about that."

"And?"

Marianna sat back, munching the last bite of salad. She swallowed, took a sip of water, then said, "I hate to admit it, but you're probably right. I don't want to, but I guess I'll be staying at my parents' longer than I thought."

"What's your hesitation?"

"I've fought so hard to be..." Did she really want to share this with him? A man she'd known for only a little over a week and met under extreme circumstances? Yet, there was something about him that pulled her, drew her to him.

He finished the sentence for her. "...independent?"

She nodded, guilt hitting her hard. Her family was so wonderful, yet they had a way of being a little smothering sometimes.

"They just want to make sure nothing happens to you."

Marianna straightened, agitation making her words sharp. "I can take care of myself. I don't need someone watching to make sure nothing happens to me."

Something flashed in his eyes. Hurt, anger, grief? She couldn't place the emotion she saw but wondered at the cause.

Abruptly, he said, "Okay, so this guy that broke in. His shoe print is different than the one we found from the murder."

Marianna blinked but allowed the topic shift. "Does that mean it was two different people?"

"No, not necessarily. He could have just worn a different pair of shoes this time. We did rule out Suzanne's ex-boyfriend, Bryson James. He had an alibi, plus his shoe size is about a size and a half too small for the print we found. That's too much of a difference to suspect him."

"What about the two prints from the different incidents. Are they the same size?" Marianna wondered.

"No, but there's only about a half size difference. Which, again, doesn't mean much. Some people buy their shoes according to fit and feel, not size. But the difference is small enough that we can't rule out it's the same person."

"So, basically, we know nothing."

"That's it in a nutshell."

"And there wasn't any DNA or anything found either time?"

"Still waiting on that. And you can't think of anything you might have that this guy could be after?"

Marianna threw her hands up. "No. I can't think of a thing."

"Well, my guess is that he didn't get whatever he was looking for Friday night."

She looked up at him, fear flowing freely. "So, I guess that means he'll be back, huh?"

SIX

Monday morning Marianna hurried to school, anxious for the day to be over so she could see Twister. She'd missed his comforting presence. Joseph had volunteered to pick up the dog for her and have him waiting at her parents' house since she had basketball practice this evening. Twister would greet her when she walked in the door later tonight.

After she and Ethan had finished eating the day before, he'd driven her home to retrieve some of her things and taken her to her parents' house. Her mom welcomed Marianna like a long-lost child even though she had just spent Saturday night there, while her father's furrowed gray brows told her he worried silently.

In the classroom she flipped on the television so the kids could watch the morning news. It was filled with mostly political happenings owing to the upcoming election, and her students found it fascinating to be informed of the latest in the process. Oh, they didn't understand it in detail, but they knew it was a big deal and therefore wanted to be involved. Marianna was happy to oblige. She and the other teachers had even arranged to have a mock election day for the entire school, with several voting booths loaned to the school by the local voter's registration office. The workers had agreed to volunteer and run the day like a normal voting day, even having the students register to vote just like any other citizen.

The only difference was no one had to meet the age requirement. Everyone was really excited about it, even the staff members.

Josh entered the room and handed over another computer part. Marianna went to her desk, pulled open the drawer and realized she'd left his box in the other teacher's classroom. Making a mental note to get it later, she dropped the part into the drawer and said, "Thanks, Josh."

"Welcome," he signed. Then looked at the television. His eyes went wide and he signed, "Daddy!"

"What?" Marianna glanced up at the screen and noticed a well-dressed man in his mid-forties speaking to the reporter to his right.

Josh jumped up and down, causing the room to shake, his large frame causing the effects of a small earthquake. Books tumbled from the shelves, and the desks danced across the floor. Marianna went to him and laid a hand on his arm. "Josh, calm down." Josh stopped but didn't take his eyes from the television.

"Daddy," he signed again.

Sure enough, that was his father. Marianna had met the man only once at the beginning of the year. The campaign manager for one of the gubernatorial candidates, he would be campaigning from Charleston this week, only about three hours away. Marianna wondered if the man would try to make it down to visit Josh before heading off to the next city on the list. Hmm, probably not or she would have been notified by now. Closed captions played at the bottom, displaying the conversation taking place between the reporter and Josh's father.

No wonder Josh lived with his grandparents. His father was a busy man, and his mother had died a few years ago.

"...overhead transparencies?"

The question came from the door, catching Marianna's attention with the noise. Misty Williams, late twenties, tall, red hair, green eyes. And a teacher with an attitude. Why the woman had taken a dislike for Marianna was beyond her.

"I'm sorry?"

Misty rolled her eyes, then stomped into the room to pull open a file cabinet.

Marianna felt her jaw drop but swallowed her desire to snap the woman's head off. As if she didn't have enough stress in her life right now without adding Misty's nastiness to it.

"Excuse me." Marianna stepped forward and placed a hand on the drawer. The woman's gall was unbelievable.

Misty stopped her search. "Transparencies. Jean said you have some."

Marianna sighed. Perhaps if she kept her cool, one day Misty would reveal why she disliked Marianna so much. "Sure, Misty, how many do you need?"

"Four or five should be fine."

Handing them over, she tried to see beyond the anger— and saw nothing but the raw emotion directed solely at her. She shivered. Why did the woman display such malice toward her?

Misty snatched them and left without a word of thanks.

Shaking her head, Marianna welcomed the rest of her class as they filed in. Her assistant hurried through the door and tossed her lunch bag on her desk. "Sorry I'm late—my car wouldn't start this morning, so I had to catch the bus."

"No problem, I'm just glad you made it." She placed a hand on the woman's arm, glanced around to see that the students' attention was on the news and asked, "Dawn, do you know why Misty is so hateful to me?"

Dawn's eyes went wide, then her lips thinned. "No, but I've noticed her attitude toward you."

"She seemed friendly enough initially, after she first started working here a couple of months ago, but something definitely happened to put her off of me, that's for sure."

"I don't know, but I'll keep my eyes and ears open for you."

"Maybe I should just ask her."

Dawn shrugged. "I guess you could. Or maybe it's just a phase and she's having a couple of bad weeks. Who knows?"

"Maybe."

And then there was no more time to worry about the situation. Soon, Marianna found herself caught up in the business of teaching and the endless stack of paperwork that went with it.

Before she knew it, the day had passed and the final bell had rung. Basketball practice wasn't until after supper, so Marianna stayed late working on papers. Around five o'clock, she pulled a frozen dinner from her dorm-sized refrigerator and walked toward the teacher's lounge to zap it in the microwave.

As she stepped from her well-lit classroom into the dark hall, she noticed how empty the building was.

Empty and spooky.

She didn't need her imagination to fill in what could happen to a lone female in a deserted building. She paused, trying to decide whether to keep going or turn around, grab her purse and get out. Which was silly, because she'd done this routine of staying late ever since basketball season started. Only now, with Suzanne's death and the break-in...

Adrenaline kicked in as she relived the terror of seeing Suzanne lying lifeless on the floor, of being alone in her house, grief stricken and weary, then terrorized once again when the intruder climbed through her bedroom window.

Returning to the scene of the crime.

Fear seized her, cramped her stomach as a terrifying idea flashed through her mind.

What if Suzanne was not only in the wrong place at the wrong time, but also was the wrong person?

What if the killer originally thought Suzanne was Marianna, learned of his mistake, and Friday night was his idea of trying to finish the job?

Ethan sat at his desk, flipping through the case files, his mind about as alert as mush. He couldn't keep his thoughts focused as he worried about Marianna. For some reason he couldn't convince himself that this last break-in was unrelated to Suzanne's murder.

He glanced at the clock. Almost five thirty. Catelyn had left forty-five minutes ago to meet up with Marianna's sister Alissa.

Marianna had basketball practice with her team at six, but no doubt she would head over to the gym early to make sure everything was ready. Tapping his pen against his chin, he thought. Should he go over just to check on her? What if something happened to her while he sat here worrying about her?

She's a big girl, O'Hara—she doesn't need you checking up on her.

But his mind kept playing the "what if" game. What if there was something behind her and she didn't hear it? What if someone tried to warn her of the danger coming and...

Stop it!

Although...what would it hurt? Just run by, say hey, and then head home. To his empty apartment. Where he would grill chicken for one. Fix one glass of iced tea. Set one place at the table. Growing up, he and Ashley had shared thousands of meals together, just the two of them, while their parents traveled the world, jet-setting with their country club friends.

Ah, Ashley, sweet sister, even after almost three years, I still miss you terribly at times.

He let his gaze slide to the picture on his desk, the last one he'd taken of Ashley. She had her long dark hair pulled up into a messy ponytail, had on sweats and a ball cap. Her grin pierced him as he remembered the last time he'd seen her, tried to warn her about the car speeding toward her.

She hadn't heard him. Instead she'd hurried toward him, stepping into the path of the vehicle. And he'd been unable to do anything about it. To stop it. His fault...

Ethan slapped the picture facedown, stood and gathered his leather jacket. He'd just go by the school and see

Marianna, make sure she was all right. But he sure wouldn't tell her that was his reason for stopping by. She was certainly little Miss Independent.

And she was probably fine, but what could it hurt? Just to see. To reassure himself.

Marianna hurried up the walkway to the dark gym. Puzzlement made her frown. Where were the lights? Her assistant coaches and student helpers?

Granted, the players wouldn't show up for another fifteen, twenty minutes, but everyone else should be here by now. Reaching the heavy glass doors, she saw a sign:

Basketball practice has been canceled.

"What?" She hadn't canceled practice! Well, that explained why no one was here. Had someone decided to play a practical joke on her? It was too early in the year for an April Fool's Day prank. They'd gotten her good last year: every one of her starting players had texted her claiming to be sick and unable to attend the big play-off game. She still hadn't come up with an appropriate retaliation.

She pulled on the door. Locked. Digging in her pocket for her key, she opened it and stepped inside.

Great, another dark hallway.

She slapped at the light switch on the wall. Nothing.

Weird.

Now she started to get that feeling in the pit of her stomach that told her something wasn't right. The same feeling she'd had when she'd first seen her door standing wide open the day of Suzanne's murder.

Invisible fingers tickled the nape of her neck.

She whirled.

"Who's there?" Because someone was there. She couldn't hear anyone, but she could *feel* the presence of someone. A dark, sinister feeling that shot adrenaline double-time through her body.

Not again, God!

Her breath came in short, whispered pants as she slipped behind a display board for the moment. She had to make a decision, but her brain felt as if someone had used the remote to put it on pause.

What to do?

Think, Marianna, think!

Her BlackBerry. She slapped her side...and felt nothing. She'd left it charging in her classroom.

Although the darkness pressed in, she wondered if she could use it to her advantage. She knew the layout of the building. Hopefully, whoever was in here with her didn't.

With what she prayed were silent steps, she slowly moved her sneaker-clad feet toward the inner door of the gym. If she could get inside the storage room, she could lock herself in.

Tears threatened as her fear mounted. But she kept her cool and took another step. And another. The door to the court lay just beyond her. One more step and her fingers brushed the cool metal. She knew it would clang loudly as soon as she pushed it inward. She'd have to move fast once inside the door.

With another prayer and a deep breath, she gave it a shove and rushed in, spinning to the left. Pure darkness pushed against her eyes. Silence thundered in her ears, even as her hearing aids picked up heavy footsteps behind her.

Trailing her fingers along the wall, she moved as quickly as she dared.

Almost there.

If memory served her right, she needed to go only a few more feet after she passed the bleachers. Praying the room would be unlocked when she got there, she kept moving. The wall ran out, her shin hit the lowest bleacher and she flinched but ignored it.

Then she felt him, her, it.

Breathing on her neck. Smelling of stale cigarette smoke. She turned to flee.

Pain ripped through her scalp and down her neck as a rough hand gripped her ponytail in a vise.

She screamed, tears leaking down her cheeks.

"I'm deaf! I can't hear you if you're talking!"

The hand shoved against the back of her head, and she went down, cracking her cheek against the edge of the wooden seat.

Marianna screamed again.

SEVEN

Hand on the gym door, Ethan paused. Darkness greeted him. He frowned, his gut shouting at him that something was wrong.

Had she canceled practice? The sign on the door said she had. He grabbed the handle and pulled. Locked.

Unclipping his phone from his belt, he sent a text to Marianna's BlackBerry. "Are you having practice tonight? I'm at the gym and no one's here. You okay?"

Anxiety caused sweat to bead on his brow. Should he call for backup?

But backup for what, canceled basketball practice?

The comfortable weight of his gun rested snugly under his left arm. He reached up and loosened the strap but didn't pull the weapon out...yet.

Retracing his steps, he climbed back into his car and drove around to the girls' dormitory, located within sight of the gym.

Several stood outside talking, signing fast, using a word every now and then that Ethan didn't understand. Must be slang he wasn't up to date on.

When they spotted him, the conversation ceased. Ethan looked around for a dorm parent and spotted her talking to one of the girls near the door to the building.

The girl she was talking to pointed to him and the woman turned, frowning. "May I help you?" she signed.

"I'm sorry to bother you, but I was looking for Marianna Santino. I thought she had basketball practice right now, but there's no one in the gym. Do you know where I can find her?"

One of the teens signed, "Basketball practice was canceled."

Ethan signed back, "Did Ms. Santino say why?"

"No, just that it was canceled."

That still didn't sit right with Ethan. "You talked to her?"

The girl nodded. "On the TTY." The telephone device used by the deaf to type messages back and forth. Just like texting, but the TTY used a landline, and the person could read the message as it was being typed out.

"And you're sure it was Marianna?" he asked.

A shrug. "That's what the person typed."

Ethan touched the tips of his fingers to his mouth and brought his hand down, palm up. "Thank you."

"Welcome."

Walking back to his car, he checked his phone. No response to his text to Marianna. His gut tightened. Not necessarily alarming, but unusual. And in light of recent events...

Should he check her classroom or go back to the gym once more? Should he call campus security and see if they'd had any report of a disturbance?

He glanced at the gymnasium and thought he saw something move. Lights dotted the campus at night, lighting the walkways and streets, but there were still spots that remained dark, places someone could hide.

The movement caught his eye again, and he moved toward it, hand on the butt of his gun.

Marianna lay against the floor, not daring to move. Her fingers gripped the object her attacker had shoved into her hand before releasing her.

Slowly her senses returned, and she felt warm wetness flowing from the throbbing gash on her cheek, absentmindedly wondering if she'd need stitches.

Every muscle tense, she concentrated on the floor. About a minute earlier, she'd felt the person move away from her, fleeing feet pounding across the surface, the vibrations under her prone body growing fainter with each step.

Dare she pray it was over? How long should she stay there? Should she try to leave and get help?

A light flickered in front of her. The terror returned full force, and she scrunched down into a little ball, not wanting to move and take the chance on making noise that would draw attention to her.

The light passed over her. More running feet, headed in her direction. She scrambled to her feet, adrenaline flowing, anger surging. This time she'd fight back and with fists still knotted, tightly clenched. Ignoring the throbbing pain in her cheek, she tried to remember every self-defense move Joseph had taught her.

Then she was staring into Ethan O'Hara's worried face as he turned the light on himself to show her who was there.

Her muscles wilted, pulling her back to the floor she'd just risen from, and she burst into tears.

Ethan had never felt such murderous rage as he did at that very moment. Not even toward the two teens who had drag raced in the high school parking lot, their irresponsible actions leading to his sister's tragic death. Ashley's death had been an unintentional act.

This, though, this attack on Marianna had premeditation written all over it. He sat on the floor beside the sobbing woman and gathered her into his arms. More beams of light entered through the door held open by the officers Ethan had called when he realized the lights in the gym didn't work.

Campus security arrived and everyone began talking at once.

The young man in his mid-thirties who held the title of head of campus security, Kevin Manning, sat on his haunches, pushed his cap back on his head and asked, "She all right?"

Through gritted teeth, Ethan muttered, "Does she look all right?"

Kevin's expression didn't change although his eyes sharpened. He ignored Ethan's question. "I'll need her to tell us what happened just as soon as she gets it together."

Ethan thought about putting his fist together with the man's nose, but reined in the impulse. The guy was just doing his job. He had the safety of all the residential students and staff on his shoulders. Of course he would need information as soon as possible.

Marianna pulled away from him, and his arms immediately missed her slight form. Using the heel of her palms to swipe the tears from her face, she squared her jaw and looked at him. He flinched when he saw the gash on her cheek, the blood on her face, smeared and still seeping. He made sure his face stayed illuminated by one of the flashlights. She said, "I want this person caught."

"Do you remember anything about him? Did you see him?"

"No, it was pitch-black. But I *felt* him." She shuddered and the tremble went straight to his heart. Then he felt guilty. Once again, someone he cared about had been hurt. If only he'd come to check on her earlier; if only…

His fault…his fault…

Shrugging those memories aside, he told himself to focus. "Did you notice anything about him? Did he have on a mask? Come on, Marianna, give me something to work with."

Overhead lights came on, slowly brightening in intensity as they warmed up. Flashlights flicked off, and Ethan finally got a full look at her face, noticing the gash on her cheek looked worse in the glaring brightness.

"We need to get you to a doctor to check that out." He reached out a hand as though to touch it, and she flinched away from him. His hand dropped.

"He…pushed me into the bleacher and…"

Ethan pulled out a clean handkerchief and pressed it to the

wound. "I think it's slowing down, but you may need a stitch." He backed up a bit and turned to see paramedics coming through.

Ethan glanced at Kevin, who shrugged. "Didn't figure it would hurt anything to call them."

Respect for the man went up a notch. "Good move. Thanks."

Marianna fought the idea of going to the hospital. "Just put a butterfly bandage on it and it'll be fine."

One of the paramedics said, "If you insist, but you still might want to have a doctor look at it. It may need a stitch or two. If you don't get it taken care of, you might end up with a scar."

She nodded and Ethan vowed to see she took care of it.

Finally, after all the commotion calmed down, the statements had been taken and the gym closed off so crime scene staff could do their job, Ethan said to Marianna, "I'll give you a ride to your parents' house."

"That's all right. I have my car."

"Then I'm following you home."

At first he thought she would protest; then she gave a weary nod and headed for the exit.

Before she could place her hand on the door, it burst open and a young teenage boy exploded through. Spotting Marianna, he broke into a flurry of signs. Her face paled and she looked at Ethan. "Did you understand what he said? Someone vandalized my car!"

Grim, jaw tight, he nodded. "Let me call the police back."

"Why would someone do this? What did I do? Who hates me so much? What is going on?"

Stunned, Marianna could only stare in disbelief. Every window in the little red Honda gaped as if it, too, were shocked at the violence perpetrated on it. Glass lay shattered on the ground around the perimeter of the vehicle. Sickness swirled in her stomach. The glass was on the outside. Someone had kicked the windows out...from the inside.

"Seems to me trouble keeps following you, little lady."

Marianna read the policeman's words, her brain on auto-pilot as it took in the shapes formed by his lips. Her hearing aids picked up some of the sounds and she processed his sentence.

"No kidding," she muttered.

Grateful for Ethan's supporting arm around her shoulders, she leaned into his embrace. It appeared that was going to be his job tonight, holding her upright.

The officer spoke again. "We'll let the investigative team haul the car down to the lab, since you're concerned this may be in connection with that other woman's murder."

Weariness like nothing she'd ever felt before made her light-headed. She must have sagged slightly, because Ethan's arm tightened. He turned her to face him and said, "We need to get you home. There's nothing more you can do here."

With a grateful heart, she allowed him to lead her toward his car, then stopped abruptly when she remembered the paper.

"Oh, no!"

Ethan looked alarmed. "What? Are you okay?"

"No! He shoved something in my hand. What did I do with it?" She opened both hands, palms up, and there it was, still in her right hand, crunched and crushed into a flat mess. Her fists had been clenched the entire time, she realized, even when she'd used the heel of her palms to wipe her tears and the blood from her face. Dried, dark streaks still stained her skin.

He sucked in a deep breath. "Hold on. Just...don't do anything with it yet." Turning, he hollered over his shoulder. "Hey, Henry, you got a pair of gloves and a plastic bag on you?"

Henry hurried over, a frown on his slightly pudgy face, which hadn't seen a razor in a while. "Of course I do, I'm working a crime scene," he said, holding the items out. "Why?"

Ethan took the gloves and pulled them on. To Henry he said, "Hold that open, okay?"

Still frowning, the man complied. With one gloved hand, Ethan reached for the paper in Marianna's shaking hand. Gripping it with the edge of thumb and forefinger, he held it and, with his other hand, unfolded it.

Marianna looked over his shoulder and tried to see what it said, but it was too dark. Ethan moved about ten yards to his right and held it up to the light. She watched his lips as he read aloud, "Keep your mouth shut, or else."

EIGHT

Exhausted, worried, frustrated by the lack of progress on the case, Ethan had fallen into bed after making sure Marianna was safely ensconced in her family's care. Her mother had seen Marianna's cheek and immediately ushered her off to examine the wound. Now, he lay sleepless once again, staring at the ceiling. Slowly, his body relaxed and he drifted.

The bright sun pounded the asphalt, sending heat waves radiating over anyone brave enough to expose himself to it. May wasn't supposed to be this hot, he remembered thinking.

Then he was in the huge, almost deserted parking lot, waiting for Ashley. Somewhere in his sleep-fogged brain, he knew he was dreaming, yet hope remained that this time the ending would be different.

As he watched his Camaro pull under the lone tree providing the only shade in the entire parking lot, he told himself to park in a different spot. Suddenly, he was behind the wheel, watching, still waiting, clueless. He told himself to crank the car and drive off, move, park anywhere but there.

Instead, he just sat there.

The familiar blue hatchback pulled in and parked about forty yards away. The occupants couldn't see him positioned as he was behind the tree.

Drive over there! he tried to order himself.

His dream self didn't hear.

Now, the events started clicking, one after the other, only now he was a spectator watching a movie. One he'd seen before and didn't like, didn't want to watch again, not if he couldn't rewrite the ending.

Ashley stepped from the car and looked around. Two other girls clambered from the backseat. One headed for the building; the other walked backward, signing, talking to Ashley. Ashley finally spotted him under the tree.

She waved to him and he waved back. She turned to say goodbye to her friend.

Engines revved.

The sound caught his attention because it seemed close.

But he kept his eyes on his sister, still walking backward, talking, signing, laughing. Grabbing a few last words.

Tires screeched as the black, low-slung Mustang hurled into the parking lot through the open gate. Its white twin followed seconds behind.

The dream seemed to slow, the camera panning back and forth between him and Ashley and the racing cars. Back to Ashley. Laughing, waving, long hair swinging around her face as she turned to run toward Ethan.

Fresh horror, remembered agony of what was to come screamed at him.

Ashley! Stop!

Still laughing, running toward her rock, the one person she could count on. Her stability in a silent world.

No! Look out! The words echoed in his mind even as he saw himself screaming at her, his shout falling on her deaf ears, sliding away.

Desperately, he tried to wake up.

Screeching tires, burning rubber.

The thud.

Ashley!

He ran to her, grabbed her, looked into her face. But it wasn't Ashley this time. Marianna's features mocked him, her eyes fixed on his but empty of the vibrant life that so defined her.

Terror and grief had him screaming out his denial. Once again, he'd failed. It was his fault...his fault....

Gasping, he sat up in bed, panting, his chest aching, the tears falling, great heaving sobs escaping. And he let them. Even after three years, the dream made the loss fresh, brought back the crushing pain of Ashley's death...and the guilt that plagued him.

If only...

Only this time, he'd failed Marianna, too.

He rolled off the bed, knelt on the floor, ignored the sweat dripping from his brow and leaned his head against the mattress. *Father, please, help me keep my focus on You. I know You don't blame me for what happened to Ashley, but no matter what I do, I can't forgive myself. I also know I've been a little slack in coming to You with my problems lately. For that I'm sorry. Forgive me, God. Help me deal with what's going on in my crazy head and mixed-up job. And Marianna...God, that's a tough call. I'm not even sure what to pray here, except to ask that You watch over her. And please don't ask that I be the tool You use to do it. I failed Ashley, God. I failed that poor woman who died on my watch.... I can't go through that again.... Please don't ask me to.*

He didn't bother adding an Amen to the end of his prayer. He had a feeling the conversation was far from over. The clock read five fifteen. Should he call Mac, the man who'd gotten him through the worst time of his life and kept him from destroying himself and his career? Mac was overseas, working as a missionary now.

Ethan wondered what time zone Mac was in, then sighed. No, no sense in both of them being awake. No need to bother Mac when he couldn't do anything but worry about Ethan. It would drive the man nuts knowing that Ethan might need his help and be unable to provide it. No, he'd have to deal with this one on his own.

Unfortunately, there'd be no more sleep tonight; might as

well work on the case…cases. Suzanne's murder, Marianna's attack, the car vandalism, everything. Somehow, when he connected all the dots, he was going to come up with the big picture of how all these separate incidents were related.

Before Ethan had gone to bed last night, he'd called and filled Catelyn in on the night's events. Her comment had been, "How is it I'm never with you when all this stuff keeps happening?"

"Because it keeps happening after we're off the clock."

"So, why do you keep clocking back in?" Her voice had been low, knowing. She'd always been good at reading people.

"Lay off, Cate, she needs help."

"Hey, I'm not fussing."

His mind's eye pictured her pointing a finger at his nose as she said, "But you'd better call if you find yourself in trouble. I don't care what time it is, on the clock, off the clock, whatever. You hear me?"

Saluting the phone, he'd said, "Yes, ma'am."

"Good, glad we got that straight."

"I'm supposed to meet her after she gets out of school. Once again, I want to find out if she remembers anything else from any of the incidents, especially the one last night."

"Let me know what she says. Listen, I've got class—gotta run. But call me if you need me, seriously."

He knew she meant it. And she knew he'd call if he needed her. That's what good friends and partners were for. And that's all it was between them. Once upon a time, they'd tried for something more, but both had quickly realized they were only meant to be friends—period.

Ethan had been disappointed at first, then grateful. Now as he thought about Marianna, he wondered what God was doing in his heart and if, after all the craziness was done, God had something in mind for Ethan and Marianna. The thought made him a little…antsy.

Right now, he didn't have time to explore that weird

feeling. His phone buzzed as he pulled open the door to his car.

He glanced at the number and his heart chilled once again. Six ten in the morning and Marianna was texting him.

Uh-oh, that couldn't be good.

Marianna kept her eyes glued to the television, absorbing the news, the shock sending shivers through her body.

Josh's father had been killed in a car wreck. The station went to a commercial. Her fingers flew over her BlackBerry keypad as she texted the message to Ethan that she wouldn't be able to meet him today. Already she was making plans to be the one to drive Josh home to his grandparents. She knew they'd want him there, especially for the funeral. And she planned to be there for him, too.

When the station came back from the commercial, she read the captions unable to tear her eyes from the breaking news story. The reporter announced, "Roland Luck, campaign manager for Clayton Robertson, was killed in a car wreck early this morning. Roland apparently lost control of his car soon after leaving a private meeting at a secluded resort atop Breakaway Mountain, just twenty-five miles north of Asheville, North Carolina. His car swerved over the side and crashed into the wooded area below. His body has been recovered. For now, Steven Marshbanks, Roland's assistant, will take over the campaign management until a replacement is named. Mr. Marshbanks is currently unavailable for a statement. We'll have more details as they become known."

With hands shaking, Marianna closed her eyes. *Lord, what is going on? My world is spinning out of control, and the only thing I know to do is hold on to You and pray You make everything work out how it's supposed to. And poor Josh, I don't even know if he'll understand what's happened. Just...help me, Lord. Wrap us all in Your strength.*

She felt a hand on her shoulder and turned. Her mother stood there, concern in her gentle brown eyes, her apron already tied around her ample waist. Maddelena signed, "What's wrong, honey?"

Marianna hadn't realized she been crying until her mother's soft fingers reached up to wipe a few tears from Marianna's cheeks. She flinched when the woman brushed the cut she'd incurred on the bleacher the night before. It throbbed a steady beat, encouraging her to find some aspirin soon. And hide it from Joseph. He'd been asleep when she'd gotten home, leaving her mother and Twister to greet her at the door, to smother her with care and questions Marianna had only partially answered.

"Oh," she sniffed, "thanks. One of my students' father was killed in a car accident this morning."

Her mother's eyes went wide. "I'm so sorry." She gathered Marianna close for a tight squeeze, pulled back and signed, "I think we need extra prayer these days. I'm going to e-mail my ladies' Bible study group if that's all right with you."

Marianna nodded and brought her hands up to say, "More than all right. Thank you."

"Now, come eat."

A watery chuckle escaped her lips. Of course, tragedy had struck and her mother's solution was food. Right now, it worked for her. She'd need her strength in the coming few days. It was only Tuesday and already she felt as if she'd done enough, had enough happen, to fill the entire week.

Twister sat at her feet while she ate. Absentmindedly, she rubbed one of his ears and thought back to the incident of the night before. She'd purposely avoided thinking about it—one of the reasons she'd turned on the news—but now she needed to make sure it was all right for her to leave with the ongoing investigation. Most likely it would be fine as long as she left a contact number where she could be reached.

Swallowing the last of her eggs, she reached once again for her BlackBerry and typed a message to her principal, asking permission to be the one to drive Josh home and attend the funeral. Within minutes, she had a reply giving her permission. Relief flowed over her. Her principal promised to have a state car ready and waiting for her.

After explaining her plans to her mother, who promised to take care of Twister, Marianna headed to school. When she arrived at her classroom, her five homeroom students, Josh, Peter, Christopher, Lily, and Sarah, were already there, seated at their desks. The two girls had their Sidekicks out, texting. A firm look from Marianna had them tossing her sheepish smiles and tucking the devices away.

Her assistant, Dawn, stepped into the classroom, mug of coffee in hand.

"Good morning, Dawn."

"Heard you had quite an adventure last night."

Marianna winced, reaching up to touch her cheek. "I suppose it's all around the school."

"Yep. Your activities are a hotbed of gossip."

"So, is it accurate?"

Dawn shrugged. "I don't know." She gave a small grin. "Whatcha think I've been waiting to find out?"

Before she could answer, she got her usual greeting from Josh, since he couldn't stand it anymore and leaped up out of his seat. He signed her name sign, fingers shaped in the letter *M* and pulled it down from scalp to shoulder, symbolizing her long hair.

"Hi, Josh." She forced herself to smile through her sadness for him. He didn't have a clue. But then his life probably wouldn't change that much in the coming days, although he would probably wonder where his father was eventually. Possibly. Who knew what he would think, how this would affect him?

Marianna started to answer Dawn when Peter, one of her higher level, if extremely shy and sensitive students, with a rapt expression on his face, caught her attention and waved her toward the door.

She turned to find Ethan standing there, one shoulder leaning negligently against the doorjamb. Her heart caught her by surprise and did a little flip-flop before resuming its normal rhythm.

She stared. What brought him here? Biting her lip, she prayed it wasn't more trouble.

Accurately reading her expression, he gave that little one-sided quirk of his lips that did funny things to her stomach. Then he said, "After you sent me that text this morning telling me about Josh's father and that you were going to take him home, my boss thought you might need a little extra protection with everything that's been going on. He asked me if I'd be willing to take on the job."

The inscrutable expression in his blue eyes caught her attention, and she wondered at the meaning behind it. Instead of asking, she looked around the classroom with alarm churning through her. "Does he think I'm endangering the kids by being here?"

Ethan shook his head. "No, not really. We did discuss it, but his theory is that you have something this guy wants and he's only going to come after you."

She chewed her bottom lip. "I don't know whether to be relieved or scared." A half laugh escaped.

"Well, the one sure way to stop all this madness is to find out what it is you have that he wants."

Marianna sighed, then turned to her assistant. "Dawn, would you mind handling the class for me? I need to make sure everything is ready for Josh."

"No problem." Dawn shooed her out the door, taking over the class with skill.

Marianna and Ethan walked outside, where the sun shone bright, casting a deceptive-looking warmth over the grounds. She shivered, pulling her sweater tighter around her shoulders. "So you got my text about Josh's father."

"Yep." He sat on the bench just outside the door of the building.

"I'll be leaving in just a short while to take him home."

"He doesn't have anyone that could come get him?"

"Sure, but why make someone drive all the way down here when I'm going that way?"

Ethan nodded. "Makes sense. And yet…" He eyed her petite frame, and she flushed at his scrutiny. "Are you sure that's safe? He's a pretty big boy."

"He's big but wouldn't hurt a fly. At least not on purpose. And maybe if I leave for a while, things will calm down around here." A thought struck her, causing her blood to hum a little faster through her veins. "You don't…you don't think whoever's the cause of all this mess will follow me, do you?"

Ethan noted the renewed stress on her pretty face. The thought had occurred to him. What better timing than a lone woman out on the road with no way to defend herself? He definitely didn't like it.

"None of the other teachers are going?" It was really pointless to ask and go through these motions. He knew what he had to do, had been ordered to do.

She shook her head. "No, there's so much going on around here, and my principal really can't spare that much manpower. Subs are few and far between."

"So, guess that means I'm your copilot."

Her jaw dropped. "Did you say copilot?"

"Indeed." He gave a mock bow and said, "At your service."

"But…but…" she sputtered. "Why? No. I don't need you to look after me."

He smiled, hoping she couldn't see the battle raging inside him. "Sorry. You've got your own personal bodyguard for the next few days. At least until we get a break on Suzanne's case and the person targeting you. And, to be honest, my boss doesn't want to take a chance on something happening to the kid who'll be riding with you. Potential negative publicity, backlash about the department being slack and all that." She still looked as if she was in shock. He signed, "So do you want to drive, or should I?"

Two hours later, ensconced in a state van—the transportation people had taken pity on Josh's very long legs and provided the larger vehicle rather than the usual tiny Taurus—Ethan found himself with special permission to drive, Josh in the back and Marianna in the passenger seat.

He didn't have to have special training in reading body language to understand what hers shouted. Arms crossed, toe tapping the floor board, chin jutted, jaw tight, lips pursed. Yep, she was mad. In her eyes, he was tramping all over her independence; no doubt making her feel like he thought she needed a keeper. He refused to tell her he was just as thrilled with this assignment as she.

God, I remember specifically praying that You NOT use me to watch out for her. Yet here I am. Exactly what do You have in mind?

Not really expecting an answer but hoping for one regardless, Ethan drove along silently, waiting—and watching his back. Not a lot of traffic was a good thing, since it allowed him to see each and every car that came near.

"I can take care of myself, you know."

The words came out machine-gun fast, startling him into looking at her for a brief moment. Eyes back on the road, he could feel her staring at him. Quirking a brow, he tilted his head so she could see his lips. "Really? Like you did last night?"

She wilted. "Well, no. Last night was…horrible. Terrifying. I just meant I'm perfectly capable of driving myself and a student to Beaufort, South Carolina."

"Marianna, I never questioned your abilities. But who knows what this guy is capable of?" On impulse, he reached over and took her hand to give it a squeeze. "I…we…just want to make sure that nothing happens to you."

Narrowed eyes nailed him. "Then why didn't you want to come?"

Her question sucker punched him. She'd read him, his reluctance. "No offense, but I don't want to talk about that."

The fact that she let it go amazed him. "Then tell me about your sister."

Another direct hit, that one to the gut. He swallowed—hard. "Ashley was…amazing. She went to the deaf school."

"Ashley O'Hara." Realization dawned. "I knew her. The girl who was killed in the parking lot of the local high school by the…"

"…drag-racing teens," he finished. "Yeah, she'd been to a ball game with some of her hearing friends from church. They were a little late getting back, and with the parking lot almost empty, she wasn't paying attention when she headed toward…" The lump in his throat surprised him. After almost three years you would think he'd be at the point where he could at least talk about the accident without getting so emotional. If only the regret, the feeling of being responsible for…

"Oh, Ethan, I'm so sorry."

Fresh guilt sideswiped him. He dodged it. "She would be twenty years old this year."

"And the boys who were responsible? I don't think I ever heard what happened."

"It was ruled a negligent vehicular homicide. Both boys had stiff fines and the one who actually hit her served some jail time. They're still doing community service stuff."

Time to change the subject. He asked, "Did you call the school dormitory and cancel basketball practice yesterday?"

Blinking at the sudden turn, she answered, "No, of course not."

"Yeah, that's what I thought. Someone called the dormitory on the TTY and pretended to be you, canceling practice."

Anger flashed over her features, mixed with fear and frustration. "So, this person not only knows my schedule, but also knows who to call, how to call and what to say to impersonate me."

"I've got Catelyn working on tracing the phone call. Unfortunately, I wouldn't hold my breath on finding anything out there."

"I know. That call could have been placed from anywhere

that has a public TTY." She leaned her head against the window, staring at the passing scenery. Josh held a Nintendo DS game that kept him enthralled.

Unable to stop himself, Ethan reached over to grasp her hand once more. Her eyes shot to his. He squeezed, a gentle pressure meant to offer reassurance. He felt the fragile bones, the slender, graceful fingers, and he appreciated her courage as she gave him a wobbly smile and squeezed back.

Ethan returned his attention to the road. Checked the side mirror, the rearview mirror.

Made a mental note about the car coming up behind them.

And noticed it was coming fast.

NINE

Marianna registered the sudden tensing in Ethan's shoulders, his body's abrupt shift to alert mode. Wondering at the lightning-fast change, she watched his eyes, not wanting to ask and take his concentration from whatever it was that grabbed his attention.

Flicking a glance in her side mirror, she noticed the black car approaching at a high rate of speed. Instant terror blindsided her. "Ethan?"

"Just hold tight." She caught the words even though they were muttered between clenched teeth.

Ethan kept his eyes fixed on the road before him as well as the car behind him. Marianna did the same. Closer, closer. Bracing herself for either the impact or Ethan to swerve suddenly, she was almost floored by surprise when the car flew past in the left lane. Then relief left her shaking.

A breath blew out of Ethan, and she watched the tension ease from him, his fingers relaxing their white-knuckle intensity on the steering wheel.

"Wow." Marianna couldn't keep the word from slipping out.

"Yeah."

Josh continued to play his game in the back, oblivious to the tension oozing from the front seats.

"That was a government car. I glimpsed the license plate

as he went by. Stupid. Driving like that. Guy must have been going ninety-five, a hundred miles an hour." Disgust emanated from him.

"Maybe there was an emergency somewhere."

"Humph. In the form of being late for some bureaucratic meeting or something."

Marianna gave him a grin, glad she could find it now that the false alarm had passed. "Don't have a very high opinion of our government officials, do you?"

He slanted her a glance and offered a wry smile. "Only a select few."

Absentmindedly she wondered out loud, "I wonder how the campaign will handle Mr. Luck's death. I guess Steven Marshbanks will have his work cut out for him, although maybe moving from assistant to the campaign manager position into the primary campaign manager position won't be a big deal for him. Who knows?"

"Clayton Robertson will bounce back. Nothing negative ever seems to touch that guy. He oozes charm."

"Hmm...which is why he's so popular with the people, I guess." She lay her head back on the headrest. "I think all my adrenaline just seeped out. Do you mind if I close my eyes for a few minutes?"

"Go right ahead. We'll be there in about an hour."

The rest of the drive passed in peaceful silence, broken only by the sound of the video game coming from the backseat. Finally, Ethan pulled into the entrance to a small, well-kept farm. The long driveway wound around and up to the side of a large white house with black shutters.

Even in January, the grass was green, showing loving care and skill in the maintenance of the property. Two horses grazed behind the house out in the large pasture. A brown barn nestled underneath a grove of trees gleamed in the bright sun; bales of hay stacked neatly to the side brought to Ethan's mind the one summer he'd gone to a wilderness camp. He'd been about nine years old, and he and his cabin buddies had sneaked down to the barn and scattered and piled the hay about five feet deep under the loft.

They'd had themselves a blast jumping into the mess. He'd been sent home early, and his parents had never let him forget it. But he wouldn't have given up those rare carefree moments for anything...not even his parents' short-in-supply approval.

Marianna's eyes flickered open when he put the car into Park. "We're here?"

"Yep. Safe and sound." Thank You, God.

She gave him a small sleepy smile and his heart lurched. Uh-uh. She was part of a case. Don't get your emotions involved with a case.

Then he wondered what their first date would be like.

Get out of the car, O'Hara.

He climbed out and Marianna followed, opening the back door for Josh. Josh put his game away and let out a squeal when he realized he was home.

As he ran for the fence that held the horses in the pasture, the door to the house opened, revealing a heavyset, gray-haired woman in her late sixties.

Grief showed on her plain face, but her joy at seeing Josh shone through. "Joshie!"

The woman smiled at him hanging over the rail petting the nose of his favorite horse. The change in the boy was remarkable as he leaned over to go nose to nose with his four-legged friend.

Then with sadness replacing her momentary joy, she headed over to him and Marianna. "Thank you so much for bringing him home. My husband fell last week and injured his ankle, so us driving over to get Josh would have been a hardship."

Marianna reached out to hug the woman saying, "It's no problem, Mrs. Luck. I wanted to be here for Josh and you, too."

Tears welled but didn't fall. "It's hard to believe this has happened; at the height of Roland's career, too." She sighed, shaking her short gray curls. "But I guess it's not always for us to understand."

Marianna kept her own tears at bay through fierce determination. Then Josh's grandmother waved a hand in front of her face as though swatting away a fly and said, "Come in, come in. I have a fresh pot of coffee on. Let's sit down a few minutes."

Everyone trudged into the kitchen, leaving Josh with his horses. He would be fine, Marianna knew. She took note of the house as she followed Mrs. Luck. Pride showed in every part Marianna could lay eyes on. From the scented plug-ins to the plethora of pictures on every available surface. Pictures on the wall, pictures on the end tables, knickknacks, family mementos. It reminded Marianna a little of her own childhood home. Maybe that's why she liked Mrs. Luck so much. The woman resembled Marianna's mother in a lot of ways. Marianna picked up a picture of Josh when he was about six years old and dressed in army fatigues.

Mrs. Luck saw her interest and stopped to say, "That's Joshie, taking after his daddy. Roland served twelve years in the army along with some buddies of his that he went to school with. Most of them are in politics now." A myriad of pictures cluttered the table, and she wished she had the time to study each one.

"I remember seeing photos Josh brought to school for Veterans Day."

A sad smile curved the woman's lips.

"And that one is my daughter, Lisa, and her family." Marianna studied the picture framed in a simple black rectangle. Ethan stepped up behind her to look. His nearness sent a sudden shiver of awareness zipping along her nerves. When his hand rested on her shoulder, she noticed it felt…right. As if it belonged there.

Briefly, she met his gaze and noticed he'd felt it, too…and wasn't quite sure what to think about it either. He let his eyes linger on hers, his fingers gave a gentle squeeze and pressure danced along her nerve endings.

Mrs. Luck intruded on the moment as she motioned them on.

Ethan let his hand drop to hers, entwining their fingers as he led her to the kitchen.

Sitting at the round table, sipping coffee, Marianna, Mrs. Luck and Ethan chatted for a few moments. Then Marianna ventured, "Well, I guess we need to see about getting a couple of hotel rooms for the night. I know the funeral is tomorrow. Can you suggest a place for us to stay?"

"Why don't you stay here with us? We have plenty of room. All my kids are grown and…gone." Looking away, she got a hold of her emotions once more, then offered a weak smile. "Don't reckon I'll ever get used to thinking of Roland as gone permanently."

"I know it's hard," Ethan murmured, "losing someone you love. I lost my sister three years ago."

"Oh, you do understand then, don't you?" Mrs. Luck nodded. "It's really strange, too, because he had just come home for a short visit."

Mariana perked up at that. "Really? Josh didn't say anything about seeing his father on the weekend." Usually, if Josh had seen his dad over the weekend, he would come in Monday morning signing, "See Daddy. See Daddy. See Daddy." Sometimes it was all Marianna could do to get him focused back on his work.

"No—" Mrs. Luck shook her head for emphasis "—no, it wasn't on the weekend. It was last week. In fact it was Monday afternoon. It was so odd for him to just show up out of the blue like that. I wondered what was going on, but he claimed he was just here to visit, although it did seem something was bothering him." The woman sniffed and wiped her nose with what was left of the frayed tissue she held. "Well, now I wonder if he had some kind of…idea…inkling that something was going to happen to him."

Again, Marianna felt compassion sweep her. "Who knows what was going on with him? It could have simply been a bad weekend or week for him. You know how it is in politics."

Mrs. Luck gave a watery chuckle. "Well, you're certainly right there. I don't guess I'll ever know what was going through his head." She slapped the table and stood. "Let me check on my husband and see about getting you a couple of rooms fixed up."

Marianna hurried to her feet. "Oh, no. Listen, we really don't want you to go to any trouble. I'm sure you're going to have family and friends descending upon you shortly. Please, we'll just go back into town and stay there."

Mrs. Luck reluctantly agreed, and soon Marianna and Ethan were on their way to the hotel.

After securing two rooms for the night, Ethan asked, "Dinner?"

"Sure. Do you have someplace in mind?"

"Actually, I do know of a little place not too far from here."

They climbed back into the car and, fifteen minutes later, Ethan pulled into the parking lot of Lakeside Steakhouse. He cut the engine. "Uh, guess I should have asked. You do like steak, don't you?"

She grinned at him, loving the way his eyes crinkled at the corners when he was excited about something, yet a bit unsure of how she was going to react. "I love steak. As long as it has broccoli and mashed potatoes to go with it."

"I think that can be arranged. Come on." He got out and rounded the car to open her door. When he placed his hand on the small of her back, sparks shot along her spine. Wow. She was very attracted to this man. Biting her lip, she pondered that as they walked into the restaurant. Ethan was everything Curt wasn't. Self-assured without being cocky; tough as nails without being cruel. Could he also be a man with the sincere desire to take care of her without being over-protective and smothering?

Possibly. Time would tell.

Seated across from him, she asked, "What's your favorite food?"

"Definitely steak." A self-deprecating smile crossed his lips. "I wasn't entirely selfless in bringing you here."

Marianna let out a laugh. "That's all right. You deserve a good steak." She paused, reached over to lay her hand on his. He flipped his over so their palms touched. "Thank you for coming with me."

A corner of his mouth lifted. "I have a confession."

Uh-oh. "What?"

"My boss ordered me to come and I wasn't crazy about the idea. Not," he hastened to assure her, "that I didn't want to be with you, but…"

"But what?"

He waved a hand. "It doesn't matter now. Today has been a—a blessing. And it's thanks to you. I know we didn't end up meeting each other under the ideal circumstances, but I'm not one to turn my nose up at a good thing." He offered another smile. "I'm glad we had this time together and hope we have more in the near future."

Marianna didn't quite know what to say. He was being so open, so…vulnerable. She gulped. "I…I feel the same way, Ethan. I'd like to see where all this is going, too."

"But first we have a killer to catch and you've got to stay out of his way, deal?"

"I'm not going to argue with that one."

By the time they returned, it was pushing eight o'clock and Marianna was exhausted.

Ethan asked her, "Why don't I drop you at the door and you go on in and lie down. I'll park the car and see you in the morning."

She'd agreed. Now, back in front of the door to her room, she slipped the key in the slot. Then stopped. Dread crept up her spine to settle at the bottom of her neck. She shuddered at the feeling of being watched…again.

Unease gripped her as she glanced over her shoulder, down the carpeted hall.

Nobody.

Nothing.

Continuing her perusal, she caught sight of the camera in the upper corner at the far end of the hall. The black eye seemed to be trained on her, zooming in, capturing her fright.

Wrenching the room door open, she stumbled inside and slammed it, leaned back against it and put a hand over her racing heart.

A quick glance around the room showed no disturbance, everything just as she'd left it an hour and a half ago. The room was simple, containing one queen bed and a small sitting area. The bathroom sat to the left of the main entrance.

Convincing herself she was just having some post-traumatic stress after the events of the last week and a half, Marianna did some deep breathing exercises while whispering prayers and managed to get herself calmed down.

Her BlackBerry buzzed, startling her. She read, "Meet me downstairs in the lobby. Catelyn called with some news."

Sweat broke out across her forehead at the thought of opening the door and going back into the hall.

Get a grip, girl. You've fought long and hard for your independence; don't start being a wimp now.

She typed, "Be there in a minute."

Tucking her BlackBerry back into the little clip on her pants, she gripped the doorknob. Then checked the little peephole.

Nothing. Again.

Sighing in exasperation with her paranoia, she opened the door and stepped into the empty hallway. Where was everyone? She felt like the only occupant of the fourth floor.

Scurrying to the elevator, she pressed the down button and stood tapping her toe, willing the doors to open. In the gold-framed mirror to her left, she caught a glimpse of movement. Someone had come up the stairwell and stepped into the hall.

Probably someone staying on the floor, Marianna, don't panic.

The pep talk did nothing to banish the memories of last night's—had it just been last night?—terrifying ordeal in the gymnasium.

Her blood thrummed, adrenaline picked up and heart thudded madly against her chest. Fight or flight? There was another stairway to her right about ten feet away. Paranoia or legitimate danger? Her thoughts scattered like scurrying ants as the remembered feel of her cheek crashing into the bleacher shuddered through her.

The elevator doors slid open. She bolted inside.

Would they close in time?

Ethan leaned back into the leather chair facing the elevators and sighed. A cup of complimentary hotel brew teased his nose, and he took a sip, surprised that it tasted as good as it smelled. Rich, creamy and dark. No sugar.

He glanced at his watch. Eight fifteen. He'd talked to his boss, Victor Shields, briefly and the man had once again imparted orders to keep Marianna safe. Ethan wondered about the pressure. Victor didn't usually take such a personal interest in cases such as this.

The elevator finally dinged and the doors slid open. Ethan stood and smiled as Marianna stepped out. Then he frowned as he noticed she didn't look quite…right. Because she was endowed with naturally dark skin, it took him a moment to notice the stress on her features, that she looked a little pale.

"What's wrong?"

"Nothing." She chewed her bottom lip. "I don't think."

"Then why do you have a permanent crease between your brows and you're about to use your lip as an appetizer?"

Raising a hand to her head, she closed her eyes for a moment, dropped her hand and said, "I'm not sure, but I think someone's followed us here."

Instinct had him glancing around the lobby. A man at the

check-in desk, a woman and child playing checkers, two love-birds on the love seat ensconced in front of the gas logs. An overweight security officer leaned against the wall, reading the paper.

"What makes you think that?"

"I…I'm not sure. It's just…you're going to think I'm losing it."

Ethan took her hand and pulled her over to the leather chairs. "Sit." She sat. "Now tell me."

"I was in the hallway getting ready to enter my room and felt someone watching me. Then when I got your text, I came out of my room, walked to the elevator and *still* felt someone watching me. But no one was there. As I was waiting for the elevator, someone came up through the stair-well and started down the hall toward me. The elevator arrived, I stepped on and…here I am. See? It's nothing. I'm overreacting, right?"

She left out the details of what she must have felt, such as fear, terrifying memories and so forth. Ethan felt a surge of protectiveness hit him. If he hadn't been sitting, it would have brought him to his knees.

God, I don't think I can handle this.

But he would. For Marianna's sake.

"I don't know that you're overreacting. It's certainly un-derstandable that you would be a bit leery, though. However, I don't think there's any reason to call in the police at this time. If someone was watching you, he's probably long gone by now." Jaw tight, he mentally slapped himself. He should have walked her to her room. And for this little meeting, he should have gone up and gotten her, escorted her down to the lobby. "From now on, until we get home, I'm your shadow, okay?"

Protests hovered on her lips. He could see them as clearly as the painting on the wall above her head. She swallowed them and nodded. "You know, I come from a wonderful, loving family, but sometimes I felt…smothered by them. It's as if I had to fight so hard for my independence that accepting help from someone now seems like a weakness."

"Not a weakness. It's the smart thing to do when you're in over your head. So, do we have a deal?" He stuck his hand out for her to shake.

Big sigh, then she said, "Deal." Her small hand slipped into his, and he felt as if she'd just grabbed hold of his heart with a handful of superglue. He was in big trouble.

He then decided to ask a question that had been preying on him since his boss's call yesterday. "Where's your brother Joseph?"

"Huh?" His abrupt topic shift threw her.

"Joseph. Where is he?"

"Mom texted me and said he had to leave to go back to New York this morning. Some big missing person case came up and they called him back early. Why?"

"Just wondering." No doubt Joseph had some connections with the local police department and probably called in a few favors concerning protection for his sister, since he couldn't be in town to personally oversee her safety.

At least that was one mystery solved.

Now, he had to figure out how he was going to keep this woman safe and his heart out of the equation. At least for now. He'd already lost one person he'd failed to protect. He wouldn't survive losing a second. He continued, "What I wanted to tell you was that Catelyn called and said they'd traced the TTY call. It came from the downtown hospital."

"Of course. They have several TTYs throughout the hospital. No one would think twice about someone using one. That's what they're there for."

"Catelyn questioned the afternoon personnel in all locations of the phones. One worker did say she remembers seeing a man using it around four o'clock yesterday afternoon but couldn't describe him."

"What about the hospital cameras?"

He smiled. She was quick. "Catelyn checked those, too.

The only person she could come up with on the camera that might be a likely suspect had on leather jacket and a baseball cap pulled low. There's no way to identify the guy."

Dejected, her shoulders slumped. "So, what now?"

"We go to the funeral, then go home and try to figure out what's going on and what it is someone wants you keep quiet about."

TEN

In line to pay their respects, Ethan took note of the somber crowd. Friends, family and campaign supporters all turned out to say goodbye to a good man and friend. The governor hopeful, Clayton Robertson, had sent his sympathies to the family with regrets he couldn't be there owing to a bad case of the flu.

At the funeral the newly appointed campaign manager, Steven Marshbanks, a handsome man in his mid-fifties with a head full of gray hair that made him look older, gave a short eulogy. "Roland will be sorely missed. He was a good man, a good father and great at his job. His senseless death saddens and angers those of us left behind. Our prayers are with Roland's parents and young Joshua. May God grant you peace in the days ahead."

Then it was time to say their goodbyes and head home. Thankfully, the return trip was uneventful. Marianna and Ethan dropped Joshua back at the dormitory, since his grandparents felt he would do better getting back into his usual routine. He didn't fully understand that his dad was gone for good. Only time would help with that.

They returned the state vehicle, retrieved Ethan's car from the lot and headed to Marianna's parents' house. Ethan broke the comfortable silence by tapping Marianna on the shoulder. She looked at him, a question in her eye.

"What are you thinking?" he asked.

A hand reached up to rub her forehead. "Just how weird it is that in less than two weeks, two people that I knew have died."

"A bit strange, I have to admit, but I guess we just kind of have to roll with the punches life throws at us...with God's help, of course." Something he was still working on. His phone rang and he grabbed it, sending Marianna an apologetic look. "Hello?"

"Hey, Ethan, it's Catelyn."

"What's up?"

As Catelyn spoke, Ethan put the phone on speaker and set it in his lap. Left hand on the wheel, he signed the conversation for Marianna with his right.

"We got a fingerprint off the car that's not Marianna's or Suzanne's. We're running it through the system as we speak."

"Great. I guess the next step is to question everyone on staff—and the students, too—who was around that night."

"We're already on that. So far no one remembers seeing anything or anyone suspicious. But you might be interested to know that several of the lights around that parking lot had been vandalized. Marianna's car was sitting in virtual darkness."

Ethan remembered he'd had to move away from the car to the light in order to read the note the perp had shoved in Marianna's hand. He'd not thought much about it except that the school needed to put in more lights. Now he found out the lights had been purposely broken.

Someone had put some thought into this—and that chilled him. The question that now occurred to him was: How many people were involved in this attack? Was her car trashed before or after she was attacked in the gym? It really could have happened either way.

"Do they have any security cameras on campus?"

"Nope."

"Figures. All right, keep digging. Marianna and I are almost home. I'll catch up with you in the morning."

"Good deal. See you later."

Ethan hung up, his thoughts racing. Marianna's brow furrowed in thought. She'd followed the conversation well with Ethan signing it.

However, confusion flickered in her tired eyes, and Ethan knew exactly how she felt. It *was* strange that two people she knew had been killed so close together in time. But Roland's death was an accident, having nothing to do with Marianna. Suzanne's death, however, seemed to be another story.

One to which he'd like to know the ending.

By Thursday afternoon Marianna didn't know whether to feel relieved or worried. Relieved because things had been so quiet or worried—for the same reason. Ethan couldn't stay with her twenty-four/seven, so she'd sent him on his way promising she'd be careful and not go anywhere by herself except straight to her students' basketball game. He'd reluctantly agreed but promised to be back and meet her at the game.

Twenty minutes ago she'd entered the gym and that had been hard, memories of her attack pulsing full force. Now the well-lit place buzzed with more activity than a beehive, causing her fears to slowly slide away.

Breathing in the scent of gym socks, tennis shoes, sweat, hot dogs, hamburgers and soft pretzels calmed her and brought her senses into focus. She was here for the students. She could do this. *You're my strength, Lord.*

Soon her girls arrived, and she lost herself in a part of the job she loved. Becoming engrossed in the game allowed her to forget her anxiety. "Let's play, girls!" Even though most couldn't hear her, she still yelled while signing so they could see her encouraging them. A couple of the players had enough hearing that they could hear her cheering for them even if they couldn't understand what she was saying.

Trina dribbled down the court and passed the ball off to Bailey, who went straight to the middle for a beautiful layup.

Marianna clapped her hands, cheered and whistled, then motioned for defense to set up.

Then Ethan walked in the door. For five solid seconds she froze, drinking in the sight of him; then warmth filled her and she realized how much she was starting to care for this guy. The whistle blaring caused her to whip her head around, to seeing Paulette signing furiously, her teeth bared in a snarl. "I didn't foul her, Ms. S. That ref can't see. He's blind. Needs to see an eye doctor!"

Forcing herself to concentrate on the action in front of her, not the man behind her, she signed back, "Don't be disrespectful. If the referee says you earned a foul, you earned it." Then she winked and said, "And if you didn't, we'll fuss about it later, okay?"

Paulette rolled her eyes but nodded, accepting Marianna's direction.

When the buzzer signaled the end of the game, Marianna's team had won and she felt so proud of the hard-playing girls.

"Whoo-hoo! This calls for a celebration."

"Pizza!" The team yelled and signed simultaneously.

She'd promised them pizza if they'd won. She would have taken them even if they'd lost.

A hand landed gently on her shoulder, and she turned. "Ethan." Her heart beat double time at the feel of his touch, and she ordered it to quit. It disobeyed.

Admiration glinted in his eyes. He smiled. "Way to go, Coach."

Heat crept up from her shoulders. Hoping her dark skin would hide the flush she knew would stain her cheeks in mere seconds, she pretended nonchalance. "Thanks."

His wicked grin said she didn't fool him. "So, you're going to get pizza?"

"Yep."

"You have room for one more?"

An eyebrow shot up before she could stop it. "You want to come eat pizza with us?"

He shrugged and seemed a little embarrassed now. "If you don't mind."

Suspicious, she narrowed her gaze. "You found out something?"

That attractive little quirky thing he did with his mouth flashed at her, and her stomach flipped. "Can't hide anything from you, can I?"

"No, so don't try."

"But I'd want to go anyway, lead or no lead."

She gave him a smile that felt a little wobbly. "Come on, you can follow me to the restaurant. The girls will be focused on their pizza, and you can fill me in on what you've found out."

Seated in the booth at the pizza restaurant located about a mile from the school, Ethan waited while Marianna loaded up her plate with the little triangular slices.

He wondered if she'd really eat all that.

She slid in the booth opposite him and grinned. "Yes."

"Huh?"

"Yes, I will eat all this."

He felt his face flush. "Caught me."

"It's okay. On game days, I'm starving by the time everything's over, simply because I'm too worked up to eat beforehand." She turned serious and asked, "So, what did you find out?"

He swallowed his bite of pepperoni pizza and wiped his mouth with a napkin. A swig of tea chased the food. Her gaze stayed steady, waiting. He didn't fool her. A clunk sounded as he set down the glass. Tea sloshed over the edge. "Okay, I'm stalling."

"Just tell me."

"Forensics turned up some DNA at your house. A hair with the root still connected."

"And?" Anticipation mingled with fear danced across her beautiful features.

He hated to disappoint her. "Nothing back from the lab, yet. Sorry."

"Oh."

"But, your car is a different story. The guy was obviously mad at not finding what he wanted. When he busted out all your windows, a fragment of cloth was left on one of the edges."

"What kind of cloth?"

"A very small piece of leather."

"Oh, well that could belong to anyone."

"And the fingerprint we found matched up with your brother, Alonso's, so I guess we're at a dead end there."

A frown marred her forehead. "Alonso's print was on my car?"

"Yeah." He took a few more bites of pizza and looked over at the team of girls, who were laughing and chatting, signing exuberantly, oozing life. Two of the girls were busy texting on their Sidekicks. Ashley would have loved…

Don't. Go. There.

Ethan grabbed the check from the table. Marianna's hand covered his. When he looked up, the sympathy in her eyes told him that, once again, she'd read him as easily as a First Steps reader.

His phone buzzed, sweeping relief through him. "Hello?"

"Hey, it's Catelyn. The boss has called a meeting and wants you here."

"I'm off the clock," he groused.

"Not anymore. We've got a hostage situation and he wants you to take care of it."

All the way home, driving the nice little rental her insurance company had provided, Marianna couldn't get Ethan's words out of her head. Alonso's fingerprint had been found on her car. Usually, that wouldn't be something she'd worry about. But she'd just had the car detailed that very day, and Alonso hadn't been anywhere around it since then. Or so she'd thought.

Aside from her spiritual well-being, there were several things in life she considered important enough to take care of. Her dog, her house and her car. Once a month, someone from Darren's Detailing came and picked up the car while she was at work, and by the time she was ready to go home, she walked out to the parking lot and climbed into a spotless vehicle.

With everything going crazy, she'd kept the appointment as a way of keeping *something* in her life consistent. It would sound dumb to anyone else, but for her it had been important. Something normal in a world gone nuts.

Anxiety dogged her steps as she headed to her parents' home. Fingers gripped her steering wheel with extra force as she wondered whether she should confront Alonso and ask him why his print had been found on her car. Or if she should just forget it.

Okay, that wasn't an option. Maybe she should tell Ethan and see what he came up with, what advice he could offer.

But if Alonso found out, that would put him on the defensive.

Maybe he had a reason to be, she argued with herself. Marianna worried Alonso hadn't quite given up the wild friends he'd used to hang with. But even if he'd started hanging around those guys again, why would he vandalize her car? His sister's car?

She parked on the street so her father could leave in the morning to meet up with his breakfast buddies. Every Friday, barring illness or family chaos, he was up and out the door by six o'clock to head down to The Skillet.

Motion to her left caught her attention. Something on the edge of the driveway, then a shadow darting around the side of the house. Had her mother let Twister out to do his nightly business?

A glance at her watch said eight thirty. No, that was too early for it to be Twister. Besides, he would have run up to greet her.

Unease settled between her shoulders; her gut churned with anxiety. Chewing her lip, she pondered her options. Get out and investigate?

Dumb idea.

Make a run for the front door?

Maybe.

But what if someone lurked ready to pounce? And what if running for the door just led the danger inside? The darkness closed in, suffocating, igniting all kinds of images of danger, the memory of the attack in the gym.

She double-checked the locks on her rental.

Get out? Stay in? Call the police? Call Ethan? She gripped her phone.

Oh Lord, what do I do?

Then the shadow appeared at her window and a scream ripped from her throat.

ELEVEN

Ethan punched his pillow and flipped the lamp on. By the time he'd gotten to the hostage scene, the situation had been resolved. All that adrenaline for nothing. Ethan couldn't decide how he'd felt driving over to the place where a young father had taken his wife hostage until she promised to let him see their children. Ethan had been anxious, nervous, with scenes from his last hostage incident movie running through his mind.

It had only been two weeks since Ashley's funeral, and he'd been going mad sitting around staring at the wall, reliving her death. Insisting he was fine, he'd gone back to work just the day before the incident. He hadn't been on call that night, but, owing to various reasons, he'd been the only one available with crisis negotiation training. Knowing he should refuse, he'd agreed to go.

The images still haunted him.

The gun at her head, Ethan on the phone, the man yelling his demands, the woman turning, fighting, refusing Ethan's orders to be still.

The gun going off…the young woman bleeding to death on her kitchen floor.

And later, his desperate desire to know if he'd done something wrong even though everyone assured him he hadn't. But he knew what they didn't. He'd been drinking. So the thoughts haunted him. If he'd stayed away from the alcohol, would he have said something different, something that would have given everyone a different ending? He didn't know, couldn't know. But he'd made a vow never to place himself in that kind of situation again.

So Ethan had put in for a request his boss had honored. No more hostage stuff.

Until tonight.

But this time, only minutes before Ethan had arrived, the woman had managed to say all the right things and the incident ended peacefully. He breathed a prayer of thanks.

Unfortunately, he was still keyed up and couldn't sleep.

The Bible on the nightstand patiently waited for him. Instead of picking it up, he bowed his head and prayed out loud. "God, You died so I don't have to. You took on the sins of the world so I could be spared punishment. Mentally, I know this, so why do I keep beating myself up? How do I stop punishing myself, and forgive myself?"

Not getting an answer, he dressed and went for a cold midnight jog.

Marianna knew if her heart beat any harder, it would explode. The figure at her window stumbled backward at her hysterical scream. And she recognized him. Fumbling with the car door, she ruptured from the vehicle signing and yelling, "Alonso! Are you crazy? What do you think you're doing scaring me like that?"

Shock twisted to guilt, and his eyes slid away from her. Fury pulsed through her. "Oh, I get it. You're sneaking out."

The guilt left his face so fast she wondered if she'd imagined it. His lip curled into that sneer only a rebellious teenage male can manage. He signed, "You're not my keeper. Stay out of my business."

Immediately Marianna forced herself to calm down, to push aside her initial fear and subsequent reaction to it. She rubbed a weary hand over her eyes. "I'm sorry, Alonso.

You're right. I'm not your mother or your keeper. I'm your sister and I love you. I really don't want to see you get in trouble, okay?"

Remorse flickered at her words. Hope ignited inside her that he'd just go inside the house. Because if he didn't, she'd have to be a tattletale. Not her favorite role.

"You'll get me in trouble if I leave, won't you?"

When would this kid start taking responsibility for his actions? "No, Alonso, you'll get in trouble all by yourself. It's *your* choice. You're the one breaking the rules."

The word made her wince, but she didn't berate him, just walked away, praying he'd make the right decision—for once. Questioning him about the fingerprint would have to wait until she had a handle on her nerves—and her temper. If she started in on him now, the neighbors would probably end up calling the cops for domestic disturbance.

And speaking of cops...

Ethan's face leaped immediately to mind. And her heart warmed. She liked him—a lot. Slipping into the house, she greeted her folks. Her mother stepped back into the kitchen, and her dad lay stretched out in his recliner, Twister at his side and a basketball game playing on the television. When she sat on the couch near his chair, he pressed the mute button and asked, "Got a winning team this year, huh?"

"Seems that way." Twister ambled over to her and sat at her feet. She leaned over to scratch his head, avoiding the white bandage that decorated him as a hero. His eyes closed in bliss. "The girls did a great job tonight."

"Did your young man show up?"

An immediate flush made its way up and into her cheeks; she could feel the heat climbing, so she lowered her head and kept her gaze on Twister, then forced herself to look her dad in the eye. "He's not my young man. He's a cop."

That made her father frown. "I know. Have they made any progress on finding Suzanne's killer or who attacked you?"

"I think so. A little, maybe." She didn't think it necessary to go into detail. Her parents were already nervous enough about her safety. Downplaying everything seemed to be the best route to go, although with all of their experience dealing with Joseph's job, she didn't think she was pulling anything over on them. "Where's Gina?"

"Out with her friends. She's leaving tomorrow to go back to North Carolina. Her vacation time is up."

"You hear from Joseph?"

Her father snorted. "Every other hour or so, checking on you." He nodded to the BlackBerry he kept by his side.

"Keep telling him I'm fine, okay?"

Anxiety flashed and he reached over to grip her hand in a tight squeeze, signing with the other, "*Are* you fine?"

She sighed. "Yes, I think so. Alonso scared me to death earlier, but..." Marianna paused, debating whether to say anything about her younger brother's nocturnal activities. No, she'd talk to him herself, first. "G'night, Dad." She leaned over and placed a kiss on his balding head. "I love you."

"Love you, too, sweetie."

She made her way upstairs to her bedroom, thinking about Ethan. She noticed she spent a lot of time doing that lately...thinking about Ethan.

The haunting she saw in his eyes when he didn't realize she was looking made her wonder if it was a result of Ashley's death or something else. The man sure had his secrets. As if he had things he needed to deal with. His sister's death had certainly been hard, but she had a feeling his angst went deeper than that. Twister jumped up on her bed to settle at the foot of it, snout resting between his mammoth paws, but he perked his ears and watched her movements.

Stepping over to her closet, she pulled out clothes to wear to work tomorrow and hung them on the hook on the door. Turning back, she noticed Twister had shifted his attention, his head cocked, his brown eyes trained on the window. She reached to close the miniblinds and stopped. Leaned closer.

Twister leaped to the floor and moved under the window. Marianna laid a hand on his head, feeling the rumble of his growl.

A shadowy figure darted behind the bushes to her left. Anger and frustration warred within her. Alonso. She'd hoped her brother would have chosen to do the right thing. Obviously, he'd decided to go his own way, regardless of what his big sister thought.

Immediately, her teeth clamped down on her lower lip, chewing. Resolve stiffened her spine. Turning her lip to mush by pondering her next move would accomplish nothing except for a sore lip. Spinning from the window, she shot from the room, pulling the door shut behind her. No sense in letting Twister out when he was still recovering. She bolted down the steps, bypassing the den where her father now dozed, the kitchen where her mother still puttered, and out the door.

Not bothering to yell because Alonso was totally deaf, she sprinted to the bushes where she'd seen him disappear. A small skipping stone walkway led from the bushes next to the house, to the back part of the yard. Two oak trees towered over her, casting her into the shadows now that she was away from the outside lights of the house.

The walkway connected to the neighbor's backyard. Once in their yard, it was an easy jaunt around to the front of the house, where he could hop in a waiting car.

Only she was too late. The front yard lay empty, the silence surrounding her; the darkness pressing in. Clenching her fists in frustration, she retraced her steps back to the house, walked in the door and stopped.

Alonso's favorite jacket hung on the coat rack. Trepidation bloomed. Her brother wouldn't leave the house without that coat. But just to make sure...

Marianna took the steps two at a time, made a right at the top of the stairs and stopped at the first door on her right. It was cracked open, a sliver of light snaking its way out into the hallway.

She peeked in and gasped.

Alonso lay on his bed, texting on his Sidekick. No doubt complaining to one of his friends about Marianna's interference in his after-dark plans.

When the fear leaped up to grab her, she had no defense, no excuses, no arguments with which to chase it away. Because if Alonso wasn't the person in her parents' backyard, who had she just sought out in the dark?

Friday morning finally brought some news for Ethan. Catelyn had spent time with the crime lab, pushing, begging, being obnoxious—and getting results. The DNA found at Marianna's house had come back, and the man was in the system because he'd been arrested for DUI. A Gerald Chambers.

The name meant nothing to him, but it might to Marianna. Which was why he was on his way to the school to see her. He didn't want to text her and break the news to her without being there to be a sounding board for her questions. None of which he probably had the answers for. He was hoping *she* might provide *him* a few. Like who this guy was.

Texting her, he said, "On my way. I have something I need to discuss with you about the case. Can you meet with me when I get there?"

A few seconds later he read, "Sure. It's a teacher workday. No problem meeting. I'll see you when you get here."

Five minutes later he pulled up to the side of Marianna's building. She waved to him from the window and motioned for him to come up. At the sight of her, his heart did things it shouldn't be doing.

Getting emotionally involved with someone who needed protection—from him. Not a good idea. He'd learned his lesson the hard way. If you cared about someone, you wanted to protect them. And if you failed, sometimes that person died. He couldn't take that chance with Marianna. There was no way he'd live through something like that a second time.

Things had gone well on the trip to Beaufort for the funeral, thank goodness, but he'd been tense the entire time. When his boss had informed him that he was going to be responsible in making sure nothing happened to Marianna on that trip, he'd told his boss he wasn't a bodyguard. His boss countered, "No, you're a homicide detective. Make sure we don't wind up with another homicide to our caseload."

The thought of Marianna ending up like Suzanne had sent him racing to her side—even if he didn't want the load on his shoulders. And in spite of the reason he'd been there, he'd enjoyed the time with her. And he had to admit, in different circumstances, he would have already asked her out and been anxious to get to know her.

Like you're not now?

Refusing to answer himself, he finally arrived at her door, his hand raised to knock, when he heard, "And that's the way we're doing it. If you don't like it, there are several other schools here. Go work in one of them."

He barely had time to move out of the way before a short slender figure barreled from the room. She saw Ethan standing there, gasped and flushed a bright red. "Excuse me," she muttered, then disappeared into the next room down the hall.

Ethan made his way into the classroom where Marianna stood, hands on hips, lips pressed tightly, flames spitting from her dark eyes. Oh, man, she was beautiful.

When she turned that gaze on him, he wondered if he should take cover or run. Thankfully, her eyes softened, sparking something he couldn't identify but definitely wanted to explore. "Problem?"

Marianna mumbled something under her breath. It sounded...Italian.

"Come again? English or sign language, please. I don't do Italian."

A smile peeked at him from the corners of her lips. Then she sighed. "I just don't know why that woman has a problem with me."

"What do you mean?"

"She was fine when we first started working here, but obviously I've done something to warrant her wrath. Now she's blatantly hostile. I may have to report her to my supervisor if this continues."

Warning signs flashed in his brain. "Did she know Suzanne? Would she have any reason to want you out of the picture?"

Marianna blanched. "No, in fact I never once considered it."

"I'll do a little background checking."

She came around the desk to shut the door. "You had something to tell me?"

"Where's your assistant?"

"She called in sick today."

"So, no interruptions, good. Okay, here's the deal. The DNA from your house matched up with someone in the system."

With eyes wide, her jaw dropped, then snapped shut. "Who?"

"Gerald Chambers."

"Who's that?" She cocked her head to the side as though the action would help her to think.

"I was hoping you could tell me."

A hand slapped to her forehead as she walked in a little circle, processing the information. "Gerald Chambers. Gerald Chambers." Dropping her hand, she shook her head. "I've got nothing."

Frustration ate at his gut from the inside. "I thought for sure you'd recognize his name."

"No. I sure wish I did, though." She tapped her chin. "I also probably need to mention that I think someone was hanging around my house last night."

"What? Why didn't you tell me sooner?"

"Because I couldn't decide if it was really someone

wanting to cause more problems, or if it was one of Alonso's friends trying to get him in more trouble."

"It doesn't matter, Marianna. I need to know these things. Now it's too late for me to do anything about it."

She dropped her eyes. "I'm sorry."

He reached out a finger and lifted her chin. "It's all right. But next time…"

Julie popped her head around the door, catching Marianna's attention. Guilt pierced her. She'd been so wrapped up in trying to figure out who had killed Suzanne and who was after her, that she'd been neglecting her good friend. Pulling away from Ethan's sweet touch, she said, "Hi, Julie. Come on in."

"I can come back later if you're busy." Julie's eyes said that "later" would include a grilling. Marianna waved toward Ethan. "This is the detective investigating Suzanne's murder. Ethan O'Hara, this is Julie, my friend and fellow teacher."

Ethan held out a hand and Julie shook it. "So, you're the reason I haven't seen much of Marianna, huh?"

Flushing, Marianna met Ethan's amused gaze and shook her head. He grinned, shallow dimples peering out from the beginnings of his semipermanent five-o'clock shadow. "I'll never tell."

"Come on, Julie, you know how the gossip vine gets going around here. Don't add to it, okay?"

Julie turned serious. "You know me better than that."

Relieved, Marianna gave her friend a gentle smile. "I know. Sorry, I just…"

A grin cut a path on Julie's expressive, almost pretty face. "No explanation necessary. Not to change the subject, but I just stopped by to see if you were interested in going to lunch."

"Not today, thanks." Marianna wanted to spend as much time as possible working on figuring everything out. She refused to admit that she hoped Ethan would suggest eating somewhere.

Julie gave a small salute, then signed behind Ethan's back, off to the side where Marianna could see, "He's cute! Definitely a keeper, but if you don't want him, throw him my way."

Trying to act as if she hadn't caught every word, Marianna turned an innocent gaze on Ethan—who had a smirk on his face and was trying not to blush. "What?" she asked. If she didn't know better, she'd swear he knew what Julie had said.

"Guess she forgot about the mirror on that wall over there."

Marianna whirled to look and realized he *had* seen everything Julie had said. She slapped a hand to her head again and groaned. Oh, brother.

Ethan let out a laugh loud enough for her hearing aids to pick up, and she rolled her eyes.

Still chuckling, he reached out to grip her hand. "Don't worry about it. Let's go eat."

Ethan drove them to a nearby restaurant, still chuckling. He had enjoyed the lighthearted moment, glad to have seen Marianna flustered, embarrassed and able to laugh at herself—and him. It was a side of her he found extremely attractive and wanted to see more of.

While they ate, they bounced ideas off each other. Marianna insisted she had no idea who Gerald Chambers was or why he would be in her house. Ethan knew Catelyn was busy scouring every resource she had in order to find out everything there was to know about the man. Hopefully, she would call soon with some news. In the meantime, he would enjoy a few stolen moments with this intriguing woman he was coming to care for a lot.

"Cigarettes," Marianna murmured.

"Huh?"

Staring down at her plate, fork held midair, she didn't hear his confused response. He reached out and tapped the hand with the fork.

She jerked, looking up, eyes unfocused. He tapped again, absentmindedly noticing the fragility of her slender hand and the silky softness of her skin. He cleared his throat. "What about cigarettes?"

Marianna blinked, focused in on him, eyebrows shooting up. "He smelled like cigarettes."

Senses sharpening like a dog on the trail, Ethan leaned closer. "The man who attacked you?"

"Yes, cigarettes and—" she closed her eyes, forehead creasing in concentration "—something else."

"What? Think." With eyes still closed, of course she didn't hear his insistence.

Then she opened them and sighed. "I just can't think of what it was."

"Was it body odor? Some kind of food?"

She gave a negative shake of her head with each question. "No, it almost smelled like cologne, but I don't think it was. It was...it was...something I recognized but can't put a name to." She gave a frustrated sigh. "I don't know. It'll come to me. And probably when I least expect it." A quick glance at her watch had her sighing. "I guess I'd better get going. I have to be back for an afternoon in-service training session."

Ethan stood, regret filling him. Each time they were together, he noticed he wanted more moments. The time always flew when they were together and it constantly surprised him when it was time to part ways. "Come on, I'll take you back. Keep thinking about that smell, okay? And if you can put a name on it, text me."

She nodded. "Sure, no problem."

Marianna stood, stretching the kinks from her frame. The in-service training had been informative, and any other time she'd have been interested, but today she couldn't focus. No matter, it was finally over. Now she'd have to deal with the issue that had been on her mind since last night before she could look forward to the thought of seeing her younger sister, Catherina, who was flying in from New York tonight.

Alonso refused to leave her thoughts all day.

She had to know why his fingerprint had been found on her newly detailed car when there shouldn't have been any fingerprints at all, not even from the guys who'd cleaned it; she knew they wore gloves to protect their hands from the constant exposure to the harsh chemicals. Her prints were probably on the driver's door, handle and the back door since she'd gone out to her car after the guys had finished working on it only because she'd needed to change out of her teaching clothes into the clothes she wore for coaching.

Unfortunately, she couldn't come up with a good explanation for Alonso's print to be there.

And that worried her.

Pulling the BlackBerry from her clip, she texted Alonso. "Hey, I need to talk to you. Do you mind meeting me at home?"

While she waited for his response, she climbed into the compact rental. The insurance company would have an estimate on the cost of repairs for her damaged car at the beginning of next week. Until then, she had to make do with the rental.

Settling in, she buckled up and reached for the buzzing BlackBerry attached to her belt. Alonso responded, "Busy right now. C U later."

The brush-off. Lips tight, aggravation with her brother gripping her, she muttered, "Oh, you'll see me later, all right. You'll be lucky if you don't see me with my hands around your neck."

Instead of typing that message and having him refuse to even answer her, she punched in, "I need to see you now, please. If you'll meet me up the street at McDonald's, I'll buy. And give you an extra twenty for your trouble."

"See you in ten."

Bull's-eye. She'd targeted his weakness—money—

scoring a direct hit...another reason for more worry. She just prayed he didn't let that influence him into making some stupid, possibly life-threatening decisions.

Although if what she needed to talk to him about was any indication, her worries had already come to fruition.

Pulling into the restaurant parking lot, she dodged mothers and toddlers, teens and ball teams, to make her way inside.

Alonso stood in line waiting to hand the cashier the order he'd already written down. The restaurant was located near the deaf school, and the McDonald's staff were accustomed to deaf customers, which made the process of ordering and collecting food easy.

She joined him in line, noticing once again how tall he'd gotten. Her baby brother had grown into a man. He even needed a shave. Alonso shared her dark eyes, but instead of the straight, heavy hair she'd inherited from their mother, he had the thick curls of their father.

He saw her and signed, "Can we make this fast?"

"What do you need to do that's so important?" she signed back.

"Nothing." He rolled his eyes, then turned to gather his food. Marianna bit her lip. His attitude continued to worsen each time she saw him. She wished she could pinpoint the reason why.

But first she needed to know why his fingerprint had been on her car.

Sliding into the booth opposite Alonso, who'd already dug into his fries, she rested her head on her hands and said a short, silent blessing.

When she looked up, Alonso was staring at her, a faint flush on his cheeks. "Sorry."

Marianna shrugged, knowing it would do no good to lecture him. That would only drive the wedge deeper. "That's between you and God."

"So, what do you need to talk to me about?"

Changing the subject. An avoidance tactic she recognized,

but an effective one. "Why was your fingerprint on my car the day it was vandalized?"

"What?" he demanded. "What are you talking about?"

Marianna's heart sank.

Because for a brief moment she'd seen a mixture of surprise and guilt flash in his dark eyes before he slid his gaze down to his remaining food.

Under the table, she gave his foot a light kick. He looked up at her—reluctantly. His defiance speared her. Slowly, she signed. "What did you do, Alonso?"

Jumping to his feet, he knocked the empty tray from the table, drawing startled stares from the other diners.

"Nothing. I didn't do anything, so stop accusing me!"

Shouting in sign language was just as effective as screaming at the top of one's lungs using vocal chords. Large, exaggerated signs, hands slapping together furiously to emphasize words, his facial expression, body language—all of it hollered his involvement in the vandalism of her car.

He stomped from the restaurant, leaving his uneaten food on the table and forgetting to remind her that she still owed him twenty dollars.

Sickness filled her because she knew one thing for certain: Alonso had trashed her car. Now, she had to find out why.

And she needed Ethan's help to figure it all out because she no longer felt safe being alone with her brother.

Shudders racked her as one last horrible question filled her mind: Had Alonso known she would be attacked in the gym that day and allowed it to happen?

TWELVE

Ethan paced his office, staring at the phone on his desk. Another Friday night working had produced no results. Marianna lingered in his thoughts, and several times he'd had to force himself not to text her and ask her to meet him.

She was probably busy with her family. Her younger sister, Catherina, had no doubt already landed and been gathered from the airport. She'd graduate this year from the Rochester Institute for the Deaf with a degree in interpreting and deaf studies. Marianna had practically glowed when she shared that information with him. They were all proud of the young woman.

He'd spent only that one morning with Marianna's family, but they amazed him with their boundless energy and obvious love for one another. He wished...

No, he didn't want to think about his own estranged family. Parents too busy with their country club meetings and tee-off times to pay attention to their special-needs daughter wouldn't be interested in hearing what their son wanted now. They hadn't been interested when he was growing up; they sure wouldn't care at this point in time.

Oh, Ashley's death had hit them hard—he'd give them that—but they'd also almost seemed relieved that the "burden" of their imperfect child had been lifted. After all, it hadn't stopped them from their jaunt through Europe shortly after her funeral. Then his conscience reminded him: They've called you several times, and you've not called them back.

Ethan shook his head, pulled his phone out of the clip once more and clicked his way through the steps until he reached the screen where all he had to do was type the letters and he could send a message to Marianna. Would she want to meet him? He really did need to talk to her because he had found some interesting news about her ex-boyfriend, Curt Wentworth, but giving her that information wasn't a top priority. Just…interesting. Possibly enlightening.

And, yeah, he wanted to see her again.

Then before his eyes, a message light blinked on, indicating he had a new text. Frowning, he pressed the button to pull the words up, and his heart expanded with anticipation.

Marianna.

Eagerly he read her message. "Hi Ethan, I know you're probably busy, but if you haven't eaten and you'd like to join us, we're all going to Wade's Restaurant on Pine Street in about thirty minutes."

He blinked. She'd just asked him to join her family for dinner. He'd rather see her alone, have her to himself, but no way was he passing up this opportunity.

"Sure," he typed. "I'll meet you there."

"Good," she responded, "I need your help with something."

His heart drooped. Oh. She wanted to see him professionally. "No problem. I'm glad to help." And he was, he just wished…

No, not yet. They needed this case behind them before he could think about a future relationship with Marianna. If he could even consider a relationship. Right now, he had to focus on dealing with the responsibility of keeping her safe. Nope, anything more would be a mistake.

He just hoped he could convince his heart of that before he reached the restaurant.

* * *

Marianna slipped into a seat at the large round table. Sure did seem as if she was visiting a lot of restaurants lately. But when her father had declared that her mother was to take the night off, everyone had agreed and decided on this place for supper. On an impulse, Marianna had sent an invitation to Ethan asking him to join them. Hopefully, she'd get the opportunity to ask him for his help with Alonso.

Maybe after supper she could suggest he give her a ride home and they'd get to talk. Alonso hadn't shown up at home in time to ride with the family to eat, but her father had sent the young man a text telling him he'd better get over to the restaurant if he knew what was good for him. Marianna's mother sat to her left, her baby sister, Catherina next to her mother. Her father and Alonso would sit almost across from her.

Alonso still hadn't arrived...but Ethan had. He stepped into the dining area, eyes searching for her. She lifted a hand in greeting even as she drank in his appearance. Yes, she could definitely fall for this guy.

Not a good idea.

Her BlackBerry buzzed, providing a distraction and she pulled it up to see a message from Curt staring back at her. Sighing in exasperation, she deleted the message without reading it and stuck it back in the clip.

A hand on her shoulder brought her head around to see Ethan seating himself in the chair next to her. He smiled and signed, "Hi, everyone. It's good to see you all again."

After the greetings, Marianna said, "Dad's outside waiting on Alonso. They should be here shortly."

"I saw your father on my way in." Ethan linked his fingers and rested his hands on the table in front of him. Marianna felt his gaze land on her, and when he didn't look away, she knew the red creeping up her neck would soon be in her cheeks. What was he staring at?

Absentmindedly, she reached up and smoothed her hair

down around her ears, realized what she was doing and slapped her hands to the table. Why did he have such an effect on her? Why did he make her nervous?

Before she could try to figure out the answers, the waitress arrived, took their orders and disappeared again. Marianna's father came in, followed by Alonso. The curl of the younger man's upper lip didn't bode well for the evening. When he noticed Ethan, his entire posture stiffened, his lip unfurled and he sat without meeting Marianna's eyes.

Conversation flowed, except from Alonso, and Marianna enjoyed the evening. No creepy sensations, no feelings of being watched, just a nice time with her family and Ethan. The only distraction was her mental rehearsing of what she'd say to Ethan when she could get him alone for a private conversion.

Then Ethan covered her hand to get her attention. When she looked at him, down next to his leg, he signed subtly, "I need to talk to you about something. Can you get away for about an hour?"

"Yes, I have something I need to discuss with you, too."

Soon the family departed, some leveling, knowing, calculating looks at Marianna and Ethan as they walked out to their cars. Embarrassed, she wished they'd just go on and leave her in peace.

Finally, she and Ethan stood alone in the parking lot.

With his hand on her back, he led her to his car. The weather for this time of year fluctuated. Tonight was mild, so she hadn't bothered with a coat. The warmth of his hand seared through the heavy sweatshirt, causing shivers to run up her spine.

A gentleman, he opened her door and waited for her to get settled before he shut it.

When he slid in beside her, he asked, "Starbucks across the street?"

"Sure. I love their mocha lattes."

Ten minutes later, seated on a bar stool at a high round

table, Marianna sipped her drink and pondered how to approach Ethan with the subject of Alonso. She'd let him go first.

"What is it you wanted to talk to me about?" she asked.

Ethan studied her pretty features, noticing the strain she couldn't quite hide. "Your ex-boyfriend."

Grimacing, she put her mug on the table between them. "Why would you want to talk about him?"

"I did a little background check on him, and Catelyn did some old-fashioned legwork to see if we could come up with anything."

"And?"

"He's got a pretty airtight alibi for the day of the murder. Some audiology convention in New York. He was the keynote speaker, so I seriously doubt he could have come home, killed Suzanne and gotten back to his convention without someone wondering where he was for that length of time. Add to the fact that there's no airline record of him flying, and it's been noted that he was speaking to a group of about two hundred people the same time Suzanne was murdered...." He gave a shrug. "Not him, if you ask me."

"I didn't really think it was anyway. As unpleasant and autocratic as the man can be, I can't picture him a murderer."

Ethan toyed with his mug, took a sip, then looked back at Marianna. "And before he dated you, he also dated that teacher you said was so ugly to you."

Shock twisted her features. "Misty?"

"Yep. Catelyn got that information from someone at the audiology office. She started asking questions of the staff and uncovered that nice little tidbit."

"So you think Misty's hostilities stem from her being jealous of the fact that I dated Curt?"

"Absolutely."

"You don't think she could be behind the attempts on my life, do you?"

"I don't know. We know it was Gerald Chambers who was in your house that night. What we don't know is if he has some kind of connection to Misty. Catelyn's working on that one, too."

She blew out a sigh and shook her head. The urge to gather her close and hug her pulled at him. He fought off the feeling and focused on her fidgeting fingers.

Wrapping a hand around them, he looked her in the eye. "Now, what is it you've been wanting to talk to me about all night?"

Marianna locked onto his blue-gray eyes and wondered how this man that she'd known for the grand total of two weeks could read her so easily. The feel of his warm hand around her ice-cold fingers did strange things to her insides. Turned them to mush, caused butterflies to swarm, her blood to hum. Those kinds of things. Things that made her want to snuggle down in his arms and let him take on the burden of all that was wrong with her world.

Reluctantly, she pulled away, straightened her spine. No, she didn't need a man to take care of her. She could take care of herself. Hadn't she fought long and hard for her independence? Hadn't she proved she was a very capable person who could face a challenge and come out the winner?

Yes, but that didn't mean she didn't need some help. Especially with Alonso.

"I think…my brother, Alonso, can tell you who trashed my car that night in the parking lot."

Surprise lit his eyes. "Why do you say that?"

"I confronted him yesterday. I'm very worried that he's involved with some people he shouldn't be involved with. Doing things he shouldn't do."

"But what made you even ask him anything?"

Marianna sighed, scrubbed her eyes with the heels of her hands, then said, "Because I had my car detailed that day." She told him of her routine. "No one's prints should have been there."

"Well, that explains a lot. The lab guys wondered why it was so clean."

"I'd been out there earlier that day to get some clothes out of my trunk, so finding my fingerprints wouldn't surprise me, but Alonso's…"

"Maybe it was missed in the detailing."

"It was on the hood, Ethan. Not exactly a place that's going to be missed."

He rubbed his chin. "So, what did Alonso have to say about it when you confronted him?"

"He was furious. He stormed out of the restaurant. Now he avoids me, won't look me in the eye."

"Then I guess it's my turn to do a little questioning—and now isn't a moment too soon." The grim expression on Ethan's face told her Alonso was going to wish he'd stayed put at McDonald's and spilled his guts rather than face the man before her.

With mixed feelings, they headed to her parents' house, where she hoped Alonso had the good sense to be.

As they walked in the front door, Marianna noticed Alonso's favorite jacket hung from the peg. She looked at Ethan. "He's home."

"Good, let's do this out on the porch. There's plenty of light, and we won't need to get your parents involved, yet. This isn't a formal interrogation, just a friend doing a little digging."

Relief at the way he was going to handle this flowed freely, yet she still worried Alonso might think that she had betrayed him somehow by bringing Ethan into this.

Shoving aside her feelings of wanting to protect Alonso, she forced tough thoughts: Too bad, kiddo. You did this—now you're going to see some consequences of your actions.

Now, if only she would follow through.

Ethan stepped back out onto the porch to sit in one of the rockers.

Marianna went upstairs to get Alonso, asking him to talk

with her. It took threatening him with telling their parents about his recent nocturnal activities to get him to come down the stairs with her, but finally his reluctant clomping steps could be felt.

However, when he opened the door to step outside and saw Ethan sitting on the porch, fear lit up his face like a Christmas tree and he whirled to go back into the house. Only the fact that Marianna stood in the door blocking the entrance and he'd have to mow her down to get back inside kept him on the porch. She signed, "Sit down, please."

"You ratted on me, didn't you?" Fury bristled from him.

"Yes, I did. But only because you wouldn't talk to me."

"So, you called in a cop?" His large signing indicated his extreme agitation.

"Yes, I called in a cop. I'm doing this for you, Alonso."

"Well, forget it. I don't have to stand here and listen to you accuse me of…"

Then Ethan was between the siblings, his fierce expression threatening barely suppressed violence. Alonso took one look and stumbled back.

Marianna bit her lip and refused to allow herself to intervene. She'd fought hard for her own independence, struggling to prove herself trustworthy and capable, pushing her parents away when they hovered. Perhaps she'd done too good of a job and as a result, Alonso had been given *too much* freedom.

Ethan signed, "We can do this here, or I can take you downtown."

Trying to put on a brave front, Alonso bucked up to Ethan, "I didn't do nothing, and you can't take me downtown if you don't have any charges."

With one swift move, Ethan pulled the cuffs from his pocket and had Alonso's wrists shackled together—in front of him. Marianna breathed a sigh of relief. Her brother could manage to sign with his hands cuffed in front. Ethan may have looked like he was on the edge of strangling Alonso, but he was thinking clearly.

"Now," Ethan signed, "one more chance. We can talk here, or I can put you in the car. Your choice."

Alonso dropped his head, scuffed his toe against the porch floor, huffed and signed, "Here."

Ethan uncuffed him and pointed to the rocker on the porch. Alonso dropped into it.

Marianna watched Ethan step in front of the boy and ask, "What do you know about Marianna's car being trashed?"

Alonso deflated; he sagged against the back of the rocker and closed his eyes for a brief moment. Then he started signing.

"I was supposed to meet my girlfriend, Kelly, outside her dorm. But then she texted me and told me to meet her down by the little pond at the president's house." The president of the school lived on campus in a nice Victorian two-story home. Recently, maintenance had built a small man-made pond that included some beautiful goldfish.

"So, I started walking toward the pond and see this guy writing notes to a couple of my buddies. I go up to see what's going on, and the guy starts freaking out, slapping his head and walking in circles."

Alonso swallowed, looked down. "I pulled out my notebook and started writing notes to him." Most deaf people carried a pad and pen to assist in communicating with the hearing population. "He offered us a hundred dollars each to trash a car." At this point, Alonso's Adam's apple bobbed several times. "I said, sure, to count me in. Then I found out which car...and I tried to back out. I wasn't going to rat on my friends, but I didn't want to be one of the guys who..." All of his defiance had leaked out of him during the telling of this story. Both Marianna and Ethan sat, not wanting to say anything for fear the boy would clam up once again.

"But this guy shoved me up against the car and told me if I didn't cooperate, he'd...he'd..."

"What, Alonso?" Marianna asked gently.

"He'd slit my throat." The signs were slow, as though he

didn't want to relive the moment—or tell the two adults about it.

Marianna blanched, sat back and put a hand to her throat as though she could feel the blade pressed against it.

"So, I did it."

"And while you guys were vandalizing Marianna's car, this guy was staked out in the gym waiting for Marianna to show up so he could scare her to death."

Thoughts swirling, she fought to process everything, line it all up in some kind of order. "But why involve the boys?"

Ethan pulled at his lower lip. "My guess is he got caught."

"What?"

"One, or both, of those guys came up on this dude messing with your car, searching it or whatever. He had to come up with a plan that wouldn't expose him and the only way to do that was to involve the kids. If they had a hand in helping him, there's no way they would go to the cops or volunteer information. Then Alonso walked up, so *he* had to be part of it."

"He warned us about leaving prints."

"What?"

Alonso nodded. "He made us take off our socks to cover our hands so we wouldn't leave fingerprints."

Ethan explained. "If prints were found on the car and traced back to the boys, most likely they would tell what they knew about the man who hired them."

"But he pushed Alonso into the hood of the car before he made them do that."

"Which is why his fingerprint was there. And if you hadn't had the car detailed that day, you never would have thought anything about it." Scary.

Ethan drilled Alonso with his gaze. "Do you remember anything at all about this man? Anything?"

"No, just that he had on a warm-looking leather jacket and a baseball cap pulled down real low. I don't think I ever saw his face, now that I think about it. And he probably didn't belong on campus because he didn't know sign language at all."

Marianna jerked as an idea hit her. "Alonso, do you still have that money the guy gave you?"

Guilt mixed with remorse...and possibly a little relief flashed in his expression. "Yes, I felt so bad I couldn't spend it."

There was hope for the boy, yet, Marianna thought with gratitude.

Ethan caught her eye and nodded his approval, her heart warmed. He said to Alonso, "Show me where it is. Marianna, get me a little plastic bag, will you?"

Three minutes later, five crisp twenties sat in the see-through bag, ready to be processed at the lab to see what evidence remained.

THIRTEEN

Saturday morning found Marianna and Catherina heading for the downtown shops while Alonso confessed his actions to his parents. The police had pulled the other two boys in for questioning and Ethan promised to let her know if anything new came up.

In the meantime, Marianna determined to enjoy herself and see if she could find Joseph a birthday present. Unfortunately, she found it hard to focus, to concentrate on having a good time, when all she could think about were the events of the last two weeks.

And the fact that her fellow teacher and her ex-boyfriend, Misty and Curt, had once been an item—now that was just plain puzzling. Yet, she felt relieved at the same time, too. At least now she had an explanation for the woman's nastiness.

As she and Catherina exited the small antique store to head down the sidewalk, the hairs on her neck stood up and a shiver danced down her spine. Shifting the strap of her purse a little higher on her shoulder, she glanced back, to the side and up ahead.

Normal Saturday shoppers milled, spending money, strolling with children. Everything looked fine. So why did she feel...nervous? Anticipating danger around every corner? Maybe she should have stayed home.

Setting her jaw, she refused to cave in to the fear that could take over her life if she allowed it. No, whoever was causing her all these problems would not win, would not take away the independence she'd fought so hard for. Somehow, someway, she'd figure out who was doing this to her and why. *Lord, keep your hand on this, please. Put all the pieces together for us. Show us the next step to take in figuring all this out.*

In the next shop, Marianna tested the scented candles, picking them up and sniffing them, one at a time. Catherina had wandered off to check the birthday cards. When Marianna turned to put the cinnamon-bun scented jar back on the shelf, she caught movement in the mirror above the display.

She blinked. A man, head bent, studied a rack of antique fishing lures. And he had a ball cap pulled snuggly against his forehead; he also wore a leather jacket. Like the one Alonso had described the night he'd vandalized her car? Coincidence, or was he following her? Did she take a chance on ignoring the guy? Should she just see if he stayed with her or go ahead and put Ethan on the alert?

Subtly, she pulled out her BlackBerry and sent a text to Ethan. "Am shopping downtown shops with sister. Man in leather jacket and ball cap following me. I think. Can you meet me?"

Gripping the device, she waited for a response. And waited. While she stood there, pretending to peruse the inventory, the man turned and went out the door. Relaxing a fraction, Marianna decided that maybe she'd overreacted. After all, there was probably more than one person in town who owned a leather jacket and a baseball cap.

Right?

Still…she glanced at her screen. Nothing yet from Ethan.

Catherina walked up holding a T-shirt that said "Kiss the Cook!" and signed, "I'm going to get this for Joseph for his birthday."

"Joseph doesn't cook. What are you thinking?"

"That he needs to find a woman who does."

Chuckling, Marianna turned back to scan the mirror. Still no sight of the man she thought might be following her. And still no response from Ethan. She realized she missed his presence. When he'd been her "copilot" for the trip to Beaufort, she'd thoroughly enjoyed his company. Shivering, she wished he were here now.

But he wasn't.

Ethan tossed down the paper that held Gerald Chambers's information. Why was this guy so hard to find? Probably because he'd been in the military once upon a time. Not special forces, but still military. Which meant he knew how to take care of himself and stay out of sight unless he wanted to be found.

Obviously, he didn't want to be found. The lab had run tests on the money Alonso had given Ethan and come up with nothing but a bunch of prints that would take forever to identify and would probably mean nothing. The police had an APB out on Gerald and had flashed his military ID on the news asking for information, asking him to "stop by" the station. They'd stressed he wasn't a suspect, just a person of interest they'd like to talk to. Ethan wanted to show the picture to Marianna, but she hadn't returned his text yet.

As far as viable information on Gerald, there'd been nothing that had panned out. Of course they had the usual crackpot phone callers who think they see a bad guy on every corner, but none of those had been the real deal.

And they followed up on each and every lead. His boss, Victor, had been adamant about that. He wanted to catch this guy every bit as much as Ethan did. Ethan gave a wry grin. No doubt Joseph was checking in on his baby sister's case on a regular basis.

Which was fine with Ethan; he'd have done the same thing if it had been Ashley....

He also suspected that Marianna's case was the main

reason Ethan's boss was in his office this Saturday morning. He'd just come from the man's office after hashing out the information they had. And it all kept coming back to one man.

Gerald Chambers. Gerald Chambers. For some reason that name was ringing a bell in his mind. Ethan picked up Gerald's file and read some more.

High society, dated a movie star once upon a time. Entered the military against family wishes. Family. That was it. Who was the man's family?

A few quick taps on his computer brought up the Internet, and he typed in a search for Gerald Chambers. He'd already done this once, but this time he was looking for something more specific.

Quite a few pages of information were listed below his search. He clicked and read, clicked and read. Time passed before he found what he was looking for.

A newspaper article. "Gerald Chambers, son of House of Representatives member Chase Chambers, has been arrested for DUI. This comes as a shock to his family, and the senior Mr. Chambers had expressed his disappointment in his son's activities. A bright political future looks to be in question as talks of rehab centers and AA meetings abound."

The article went on to cover Chambers's military career, where he'd had a few scrapes with the law but nothing major. Then the little note at the bottom caught his attention. "It might be of interest to some that Chase Chambers did a little string pulling to get his son honorably discharged from the army and placed on the campaign committee for Clayton Robertson. It seems Gerald is headed for a career in politics whether he wants one or not."

Ethan grunted. No wonder the guy drank. He could almost feel sorry for the man except for the fact that he broke into Marianna's home. And the fact that Roland Luck, also part of Clayton Robertson's political campaign, was dead. Now how did those two facts add up, and what did they have to do with Marianna?

Because there was no way this was all just a coincidence. He reached for his phone to call Catelyn and slapped empty air.

What?

He frowned, glanced around his desk. Nothing.

Then he remembered he'd gone into Victor's office to talk for a brief moment. He'd set it on the side table, then walked off without it. He got up to get it when his boss appeared in the doorway holding the device. "Hey, O'Hara, this thing's been going off for the last ten minutes. You want to get it? I was on the phone or I would have brought it out sooner."

"Yeah, thanks. No problem." Ethan took the phone and looked at the screen. Marianna had sent him a text. Clicking on the button, he pulled up her message and read, "Am shopping downtown shops with my sister. Man in leather jacket and ball cap following me. I think. Can you meet me?"

Cold dread settled in the pit of his belly. "Hey, Chief!"

Marianna continued to shop, keeping an eye out for the man in the baseball cap. So far, so good. Nothing for the last fifteen minutes or so even though she couldn't shake the feeling she needed to stay on guard. Watch her back.

And while she enjoyed the time with Catherina, she couldn't shut off the part of her brain that insisted on going over every detail she could remember about the case. Not to mention the worry about Alonso. True, he seemed genuinely remorseful over his part in the vandalism, yet...

She sighed, and looked up into the window of the next shop. Catherina touched her arm and signed, "I want to go in there. I've got an apartment to furnish in a couple of months."

"I can't believe you're graduating from college already." She smiled. "Mom and Dad are so proud of you. We all are."

Catherina blushed, but the pleased look on her face told Marianna that her words meant a lot. She nodded toward the store. "Go for it. I'm going to grab an ice-cream cone." If she was being followed, she wanted her sister somewhere else. She wouldn't bring this danger into her life.

Oblivious to Marianna's tension, her sister laughed. "Get me one, too."

"Absolutely."

Catherina disappeared into the store and Marianna turned to walk over to the portable Bruster's Ice Cream stand. As she ordered the treat, she glanced over her shoulder. Maybe she should have stayed with her sister. The man behind the counter held the cones out and Marianna took them.

Then something crashed into her back, her feet went out from under her and she let out a scream as the cones went flying to splat on the ground next to her. Pain shot up from her hip to her spine. Her left elbow hit the concrete and agony seared her arm. She felt her purse ripped from her shoulder, saw running feet pounding past her.

Groaning, she scrambled to her feet, ignoring the aches and pains—and terror—to stumble after the fleeing thief. Then a police car pulled up beside the escaping man and slammed on brakes. The officer—Ethan?—jumped from the vehicle to give chase.

Marianna hobbled along as fast as her throbbing hip would allow. The two men disappeared into a little alley set between two stores. Hurrying, she rounded the corner and stopped. Ethan and the thief were locked in combat, each struggling to get the upper hand.

Marianna had a hard time keeping up with who was who and which fist landed where. Ethan pushed the guy off him, and the man landed on several metal trash cans. Even Marianna's hearing aids picked up the screeching clanging.

A man in an apron stepped out the back door of his restaurant kitchen, frying pan in hand, held as a weapon, to investigate the ruckus. Catching sight of the action before him, with eyes wide, the heavyset chef turned to scuttle back in, but before he disappeared, Marianna grabbed the frying pan from his hand. He offered no protests as he slammed the door.

She turned back to the battling duo and stepped forward, terror racing through her veins, making her shake. She held the cast-iron handle with a death grip and prayed out loud, "Lord, help me, please."

When she focused on the man trying to beat Ethan to a pulp, she had a flash of recognition. She'd seen him somewhere before.

Then the knife caught her full attention.

Ethan reached for his gun but didn't have time to grab it because he had to defend himself against the attacker's rush, knife held out in front of him. Ethan stepped away. The man jabbed again, slicing through shirt and forearm. She saw Ethan grimace, the blood rushing down his arm. He ignored it and set his feet to brace himself for the next attack.

Both men seemed to have forgotten her presence.

As the attacker rushed past her, she brought the frying pan up as hard as she could, aiming for his face, but her blow was off, instead catching the outstretched hand carrying the knife.

Where was his backup? Adrenaline flowed as Ethan scrambled after the perp. His arm throbbed mercilessly. Then a solid thud echoed in his ears, followed by a crunching sound, a scream of pain and the knife spinning through the air to land some thirty feet behind him.

He scrambled for his gun, then realized he didn't have to. Six officers had their weapons trained on the perp, who lay on the ground, grasping his broken wrist, screeching in agony. The ball cap had flown off in the attack, revealing a face Ethan recognized in an instant.

Panting, Ethan made his way over to the man and pulled both arms, wounded or not, behind his back. The groaning and screaming increased, but Ethan was more worried about the damage the man might still be able to inflict than a broken wrist. Especially if he was high on some drug, although the fact that the guy was feeling pain indicated there were no mind-altering substances flowing through his veins.

Except maybe alcohol. He only now just got a whiff. The man reeked of the stuff. Ethan motioned for his backup to haul Gerald off to the squad car, where they'd wait for an ambulance to come. Even bad guys got medical attention before they had to go to jail. Through gritted teeth, Ethan read him his Miranda rights: "You have the right to remain silent. If you choose to give up that right..."

One of the officers took over, pulling the guy to the waiting paramedics. As for himself, he'd get his arm taken care of, then head down the station to question Gerald. He had so many questions burning through his brain that he needed the space to organize them.

"Ethan, are you all right?" Marianna's worried voice cut through the haze of pain coming from his arm.

He grimaced. "Yeah." He gestured toward the man. "That's Gerald Chambers."

A puzzled frown crossed her face as she studied the man, then she shook her head, turning her focus back on Ethan. "You need to get that patched up. Come on, I'll drive you to the hospital."

One of the other officers walked up, and the annoyed expression on the man's face put Ethan on guard. When the cop turned to Marianna, Ethan paid attention. "Nice job with the frying pan, ma'am, but we were right there with our guns drawn. Should have let us do our job."

Marianna bit her lower lip and swallowed hard. "I didn't know you were there."

Disbelief cut across the policeman's face. "I hollered at you to move. You were in the line of fire."

Ethan stepped up. "She's deaf, Joel. Lay off."

Marianna felt slightly sick. Wanting nothing more than to go home and pull the covers up over head and hibernate for the next twenty-four hours, she gathered her courage, her nerves...and her independence.

Coolly, she glared at the two men standing before her. To

the cop she said, "Don't worry about it. You couldn't have known." To Ethan she said, "And you didn't need to pipe in and tell the man I'm deaf. I'm perfectly capable of explaining that myself."

When Ethan's jaw dropped at her dressing-down, it didn't make her feel better necessarily, but she had to make him understand she didn't need a keeper. Sure, she knew she needed help in this whole mess, but some things she could—and would—handle herself. "Now, would you like a ride to the emergency room?"

His jaw snapped shut. "Yeah."

As they walked out of the alley and onto the sidewalk, they passed the ambulance where Gerald sat receiving medical treatment for his wrist. She stopped, stared at him, read his lips almost absentmindedly as he whined his innocence, complaining he'd been attacked and wanted to file a police report.

Marianna bit her lip and chewed for a moment until a warm, if dusty, finger pulled it from between her teeth. Startled, she looked at Ethan, who stared at her with a warm look in his eyes. "Thanks for coming to my rescue."

Previous irritation melted, as did her heart. "If I'd known those policemen were behind me, I'd have moved out of the way and cowered in the corner instead."

He laughed. "I doubt you would have cowered, but the fact that you were willing to jump in and help...well, that says a lot. Thanks."

"Sure." The pitter-patter of her heart and the mushy sensation settling in the pit of her stomach goaded her to action. With both hands, she reached up and cupped Ethan's face. His eyes flared in surprise then turned smoky as he realized what she was going to do. He met her halfway and his lips landed on hers with sweet intent. Marianna reveled in the sensations sweeping through her. Then she pulled back and smiled. "Now we can go to the hospital." She turned back to the man who'd tried to do her bodily harm—again. And she studied him.

Ethan nudged her. "Hey, I'm ready for that ride and I might need another kiss."

She grinned at him and blushed, then narrowed her eyes and said, "I know him."

"What?"

"I think I know that man. Or at least I've seen him somewhere before."

"Where?"

"At Mr. and Mrs. Luck's house. He was in one of her pictures sitting on the sofa table. I remember picking it up to admire it." Confusion tagged her. "So what's the connection between Roland Luck, a dead man, and Gerald Chambers, a man who tried to kill me?"

FOURTEEN

Ethan thought about Marianna's question the entire time he was being stitched up. She'd insisted on waiting for him to be discharged, quietly staying out of the way, but her ever-moving eyes told him she didn't miss a thing going on.

Such as the fact that he refused a painkiller. She frowned as if she wanted to say something, but resisted. He appreciated her restraint. There was no way he was going to cloud his thinking when he still had to interrogate a suspect.

Leaving the hospital, he asked, "Do you feel like going to the station with me? Or do you want me to take you home?"

"Is he there already?"

"Yeah, released from the hospital and transported ten minutes ago. He's on his way to being booked, but I asked the arresting officers if they'd put him in an interrogation room so I could have a go at him."

"I'll go with you. I want to know what he says."

"If you stand behind the two-way mirror, you should be able to see enough of the conversation as it happens."

Her eyes lit up. "You'd let me do that?"

"Sure, you're the one he's after. Seems only right to me."

Ethan let her drive and breathed a sigh of relief when they arrived. Every bump jarred his wound, causing it to be one throbbing mass of pain by the time the station came into sight. It wasn't Marianna's fault; she'd tried to drive smoothly.

Pulling himself from the car, he placed his good hand on her back and led her into his second home. Her warmth radiated up his arm and he remembered the feel of her sweet lips on his. He swallowed hard at the intense emotions she roused in him. Wishing he had time to examine them, he instead put them aside for later retrieval and study.

Shrugging off well-wishing and congratulations on his collar, Ethan stayed the course and honed in on the last interrogation room on the left. Spotting a female officer, he asked, "Sarah, would you take Marianna up to the viewing room?"

"Sure."

He turned to Marianna. "Just follow her. Stay there until I come get you, okay?"

Marianna nodded and Ethan watched them disappear down the hall then around the corner. Placing his hand on the knob, he drew in a deep breath, steeled himself against the pain in his arm and opened the door.

Marianna followed the officer to a small room not too far from the door Ethan had stopped in front of. When she entered, two other officers stood there. She recognized them as the arresting officers.

Ethan had taken a seat at the lone table across from the man she now knew as Gerald Chambers.

"Anything you want to say before your lawyer gets here?"

The man's eyes flicked contempt at Ethan before he looked back at the table in front of him. His arm in the cast lay across his belly; his good arm relaxed in his lap.

Marianna could read body language as well as the next person. Probably better. This guy was not going to talk to anyone. He didn't seem the least bit worried he'd just been charged with attempted murder of a police officer, resisting arrest and assault.

Ethan tried again. "Why are you after Marianna?"

The man sighed, shifted, and shut his eyes as though Ethan annoyed him.

Marianna winced. If Ethan clenched his jaw any tighter, he'd need dental work. While the man's eyes were closed, she watched Ethan struggle to let go of his anger, his tension, to let his muscles relax. He didn't drop his guard, but he did gain better control.

His next question was a common interrogation tactic, ask questions you already knew the answer to, to get the perp's reaction. "What's your connection with Roland Luck?"

That got Gerald's attention. His head snapped up, eyes locked on Ethan. Then he smirked. "Who?"

"Roland Luck." Ethan said the name slowly as though speaking to someone who didn't quite have all his marbles.

"Never heard of him."

Ethan slapped the table in front of him, causing the prisoner to jump. He wasn't quite as relaxed as he wanted Ethan to believe. Good.

"Everybody who's interested in politics has heard of him. Don't give me that."

At this point, Gerald's attorney bustled in, a short older woman named Helen Zanislowski, with eyes like steel. Sharp, intelligent. And highly paid. "Okay, zip it up, Gerald." She zeroed in on Ethan. "You have no right to question my client without me here."

"I was just—talking out loud to myself, so to speak."

She snorted.

Ethan filled her in on the things he'd talked about thus far. "I was just asking him about his connection to Roland Luck—who he claims not to know."

Gerald widened his eyes as though recognition had just hit him, and he spoke before his attorney could say anything. "Oh, yeah, that guy who died in the car accident. Had something to do with the governor's campaign. Right." He spread his hands, or at least tried to, hampered only a bit by the cast, innocence personified. "What's that got to do with me?"

"That's what I want to know."

"Gerald, be quiet, don't say another word."

Chambers ignored his attorney. "And why would you think I even know this dude?"

Ethan leaned forward. Should he play this card now or keep it close to his chest? That was the thing about interrogations. Sometimes you just had to go with your gut. So he did.

"Because Roland Luck's mother had a picture of you, your father and Roland, all dressed in your army fatigues, sitting on an end table in her living room. Not to mention the fact that your DNA was found in Marianna's house. *And,* you're working with the same campaign. Come on, man. Get real." He leaned forward. "You're not doing this alone. Who's pulling your strings?"

Gerald's jaw nearly hit the table; he was clearly shocked that Ethan had so much on him. This time his glance to his attorney was pleading, bravado draining away in the face of Ethan's statement.

She held up a hand. "Oh please, Ethan. There are so many people involved in the campaign that it wouldn't surprise me that Gerald doesn't know everyone. We'll discuss the photo later. I need to talk to my client. If you have any more questions, we'll have to set up a time."

Ethan gave a snort of disgust. "You do that. In the meantime, I'll be gathering the rest of the evidence against your client."

Marianna let out the breath she didn't realize she'd been holding. She'd gotten most of the conversation. Speech reading definitely wasn't a perfected art, and she was better at it than most, but she still missed a word here and there, depending on the shape of the mouth, whether the person talked through gritted teeth or rubbed a hand across his mouth; or maybe as a stranger, she just wasn't used to the way he or she talked. Things like that could mess her up, but for the most part, she'd understood Gerald amazingly well.

And she'd understood that Gerald wasn't talking. What could his connection be with Josh's family? The picture in Mrs. Luck's house gave a good indication that the relationship was more than merely one among acquaintances. It suggested friendship.

Marianna decided that a phone call to Mrs. Luck was in order just as soon as Ethan could make it for her. Oh, she could always use the TTY, but Ethan would speed the process along, get the information faster.

She watched the lawyer leave. The police used special cuffs on Gerald in order to accommodate his cast as they returned him to his holding cell. The charges against him were strong; she just hoped his family's influence wasn't stronger.

Ethan exited soon after, and Marianna turned toward the door so she would be able to see him as soon as he opened it.

Within a minute, the door swung inward. He filled out the entry, broad shoulders nearly reaching from one side to the other. Would he be different? Would he be able to accept her as she was? Hearing deficiency and all? Would he be able to handle her crazy family, including her juvenile delinquent of a brother?

And why was she even going down this road of thought? He was a cop. A professional. Yeah, and one who spoke her language.

Curt spoke it, too, and she remembered how well that turned out. She trusted too easily, too fast. She fell for his charming ways and smooth talk.

All of these thoughts tumbled through her mind with lightning speed. Then Ethan was smiling, satisfaction gleaming. "I think we've got our guy."

"But we still don't know what he was looking for."

"True, but I think in time he'll spill it."

"What about his family? They're pretty powerful here in the state. Won't they have some influence?"

He took her hand to pull her from the room. She followed,

letting him lead her as she watched his face. "They'll try. In fact, Gerald's father already has a call in, but with the evidence against him, plus our eyewitness accounts," he said, flexing his arm, "not to mention the fact the man sliced me, I'd say we're pretty good. The father can argue all he wants, but the fact remains, his son's guilty."

Relief slowly eased its way through her. She was starting to believe it might finally be over. Life could return to normal. She gazed at the tall man beside her. But would life ever truly be normal? "Was he the man who made the call from the hospital?"

"Looks like it. Same jacket, even with a piece of leather missing from the sleeve. Plus it was the same hat."

"And the one who attacked me in the gym?"

"Probably." A frown caught at his forehead. "Did you smell alcohol on the man from the gym?"

She closed her eyes, not wanting to remember the incident but forcing herself to relive it. Walking into the gym, knowing someone was there, feeling his presence behind her, the breath-snatching fear, the agonizing moment when she thought she was dead. Her heart rate accelerated just thinking about it. She gripped the door handle, tuned all her senses into that moment. The smell of cigarettes, a sweet sickly, smell of…alcohol?

Instead of pondering that thought, she asked, "No, I don't think it was alcohol. It was more like cologne, a woodsy, yet sweet kind of smell. One I've smelled before and didn't like." She snapped her fingers. "Chewing tobacco! That's what it was, I guarantee it."

"Tobacco?"

"Yes. I'm sure of it. Alonso tried it once upon a time, and it stunk up the place." She shrugged. "What do you think about calling Mrs. Luck and asking her about the relationship between her family and the Chambers family? I'm guessing Roland and Gerald's father were involved in politics together and became friends. And they both had on military uniforms. Maybe they met in the army."

"And Gerald followed in his father's footsteps."

"Yes, all three were in uniform."

"Makes sense. Do you have the number?"

She grimaced. "Yes, but it's in my classroom."

"Want to ride over there and get it?"

"Sure, why not?"

Ethan walked her out to her car and opened the door for her. She climbed in and Ethan walked around to climb in the passenger side. He made only one painful face as he reached up to grab the seat belt.

"Does it hurt that bad?"

He shot her a rueful look. "Kind of like being dipped into a vat of boiling tar."

"Ack. Sorry." Definitely painful.

"It's all right. It'll pass."

The flash of Gerald with the knife, charging at Ethan, and the remembered terror. It was all still too fresh. She swallowed hard. The graze of his knuckles sliding down her cheek caught her, and she flicked him a glance. He said, "Don't think about it."

She started the car. "It's hard not to." The path his knuckles traveled tingled. Her insides shuddered, and she realized she was very attracted to this man. What would happen when this was all over? And it *was* getting close to being finished…she hoped. She fingered her hearing aid and studied him. Could it be possible he was different? Could he truly accept her as she was? Hearing loss and all. Could it be possible she'd finally met a man who wouldn't try to "fix" her?

"Ashley would have liked you."

His out-of-the-blue comment startled her. She wondered if she'd caught exactly what he'd said. "Excuse me?"

"Ashley." He gave her a wistful smile. "She would have liked you. A lot."

"Well…thanks."

"You're a lot like her, different in many ways but alike, too."

"How?" He was letting her in. Opening himself up and allowing her to see the hurting, vulnerable side of him. She remembered their dinner the night before Roland's funeral, remembered his kindness, his willingness to be honest with her about his feelings. It made her want to reciprocate.

For a moment he didn't answer, and she wondered if he was having second thoughts about keeping the conversation on this particular topic. Then he took a deep breath, "She was an incredible girl. Had a deep faith in God you wouldn't expect someone of her age to have."

"I think I remember her going on a mission trip when she was a student here."

A faint smile curved his lips. "Yes, her last one. To a deaf school in Jamaica. She loved it. And came back even more determined to make her mark on her world." Then he frowned. "That's why it's so hard to understand how God…"

"…could let her die?"

His throat bobbed. "Yeah."

"I don't know, Ethan. But I think He understands why you would ask that."

Reaching over, he grasped her hand. "Thanks. I think so, too. I finally had to come to the conclusion that if God is who He says He is, then I have to choose whether I believe it or not. It was a long road, and I can't fathom the purpose of her death, but…"

"God is faithful and just."

He squeezed her hand, then pulled away. "Yeah."

And then there was no more time to delve deeper. And Marianna wasn't sure what to think.

Arriving at the school, she waved to the weekend security guard and drove through the gate, winding around the campus to reach her building.

Two other cars sat parked on the side of the road, and Marianna's heart sank when she recognized Misty's. Great. Often teachers worked on the weekends, but Marianna hadn't even thought she'd run into the woman who continued to aggravate her. She glanced at Ethan, his strong presence a comfort.

But *not* a necessity, she assured herself. She wasn't compromising her independence by being glad he was with her. Was she? She'd come to rely on him…a lot. A niggling sense of discomfort pierced her. She'd fought long and hard to convince her family she could take care of herself. Even having a deaf mother hadn't made a difference. The woman had married Marianna's father right out of high school.

Because Marianna was the first deaf child born, they'd been so protective. Overprotective. Smothering her. Especially Joseph. He'd driven her nuts before she'd finally gotten old enough to stand up for herself. Fortunately, she'd been blessed with a healthy dose of stubbornness that had done her well when it came to dealing with Joseph.

But she didn't need to be so antsy when it came to Ethan. He was here because she was truly in danger, needed someone to watch out for her. Keep her from harm. He didn't smother her or make her feel as if she were incompetent. He didn't try to change her, force her to be someone she wasn't. He just…watched out for her.

She could live with that.

Using her key, she opened the door and stepped into the building. It smelled like…school. Crayons, markers, paper, copies, glue, sometimes popcorn and cookies. She smiled. No matter what school she entered, they all had that same educational fragrance, one that Marianna loved.

Ethan once again placed a hand at her back, and once again she shivered at the contact. Would his touch ever grow old? Would she ever not want to be with him? Breathe in his unique scent? Would the anticipation of waiting for him, watching him walk into the room, dwindle over time?

All of these questions flittered through her mind as she walked to the door of her classroom—and found it already open.

She paused. Ethan moved his hand from her waist to her

shoulder, turning her to look at him. "Should that door be open?"

Marianna shook her head. "I always lock up when I leave on Friday. Maintenance people come in to clean, but they always leave the door locked when they finish. I don't know why it would be open. No one knew we were coming up here, so…"

He pulled her back a little, then stepped in front of her. "Let me just take a look."

"I'm sure it's nothing," she protested, but not too forcefully.

"One way to find out." He stepped into the room.

Marianna followed in spite of his order to stay put.

And found Misty going through her desk.

Anger flowed and Marianna clenched a fist to keep it in check. The woman looked up with a deer-in-the-headlights expression on her face. Marianna watched her swallow, clearly incapable of speech, her eyes flitting back and forth between the two who'd just walked in on her.

Ethan said nothing and simply looked at Marianna as he stepped to the side.

And she realized what he was doing.

Since there was nothing life threatening about the situation, he was deferring the handling of it to her. Something flowed through her at that realization. In the blink of an eye she realized she could love this man.

Unfortunately, she didn't have time to dwell on that. Instead, she focused on the woman still standing behind the desk. *Help me say the right thing, Lord. Show me how to handle this.*

Keep your cool, Marianna. Deep breath. "Is there something I can help you with?"

Misty straightened, and an expression appeared that Marianna had never seen cross the woman's face.

Shame.

Misty dropped her eyes and moved away from the desk. A tear leaked out to trail down her cheek. Then she moved from behind Marianna's desk and dropped into Josh's seat. It swallowed her small frame.

Marianna glanced at Ethan. He motioned he was going to step out of the room to give them some privacy. She shook her head. If the woman said something to incriminate herself in any of the problems Marianna had been facing lately, she wanted a witness.

She moved over and placed a hand on the woman's shoulder. "What can I do?"

The teacher looked up, all traces of animosity gone. "I'm so sorry for everything." She gave a little self-mocking laugh. "I guess the old adage about a woman scorned is true."

Marianna pulled up a chair and faced Misty. Ethan stepped back, but remained in hearing distance. He'd understood why she wanted him to stay.

"You're talking about Curt, aren't you?"

Shock filtered through the shame. "How did you find out?"

"I sort of came by the information accidentally. A friend was...researching something for me and asked me if I'd known you two had dated."

"Yes, we did. For about three years."

"Oh, I didn't realize it had been that long."

"He just wouldn't commit to marriage, and I'm not getting any younger. So—" she shrugged "—I broke up with him, thinking it would send him running back to me. Be a wake-up call, so to speak. Instead, he found someone else." Tears hovered once again as she looked Marianna in the eye. "You."

Marianna ran a hand through her hair, pushing it back behind her ears. "And you want him back."

A hiccupping sob escaped the woman. "Yeah. How dumb is that?"

Real dumb, but Marianna decided to keep that to herself. "Well, we're not dating anymore."

"I know, but he refuses to get back together with me, and

I just…" Another sigh. "I just took my frustration out on you. I'm really sorry. Can you ever forgive me?"

"Of course. But why were you going through my desk?"

A flush crept up into Misty's face. "Curt changed his numbers, and I thought you might have them written down somewhere."

"Ah." Marianna reached over and covered the woman's hand. "Don't waste your time on him. You deserve better. Believe me, I know."

More tears threatened, but Misty managed to hold them back. She said, "So I keep telling myself."

"Would you like to come to church with me sometime?"

Once again Marianna had managed to shock the poor woman. "What?"

"Sure. What better way to start over. Trust me, you don't need Curt. He'll just try to change you into what he thinks you should be instead of…" Marianna snapped her lips shut and glanced at Ethan to see a gleam in his eyes. She'd revealed something very personal, and he hadn't missed it.

Marianna stood. "I'm glad this happened."

"You are?"

"Yes. I'm glad I got to see the real you."

Misty shook her head. "So, you're not going to report this?"

"No. I believe you when you say you're sorry. And I hope we can be friends in spite of everything."

"Oh, thank you!" Misty looked as if she might hug her but withdrew at the last moment and left the classroom.

Marianna looked back at Ethan, who had a strange look on his face. She asked, "What?"

"That was a really nice thing you just did."

Embarrassed, Marianna shrugged. He asked, "Is that what's called living your faith?"

She paused and thought a moment, then smiled. "Yeah, I guess it is."

"Well, I think we can safely assume that Misty is not involved with all your latest problems."

"I would agree with that." She went to her desk, pulled open a drawer and found Josh's file. She rattled off the number to Ethan, who dialed it on his cell phone.

Ethan listened to the ringing, impatient for one of the Lucks to answer. When the voice mail picked up, he winced but left a message, asking Mrs. Luck to call back because he had a question for her.

"No answer." He clicked the phone shut.

Marianna grimaced. "Well, we can try again later."

"I'll keep the number on my phone." He looked around. "You ready to go?"

"I guess. I need to check in on Alonso and see how he's doing anyway."

"Let's take Gerald's picture by and see if he can ID the guy as the man who paid him to trash your car."

FIFTEEN

Arriving at Marianna's family home, Ethan ignored the throbbing of his injured arm and the fatigue that dragged at him and found himself once again overwhelmed by the boundless energy of her family. All but her elder brother, Joseph, were gathered in the backyard, playing a game of flag football. Even her mother had on a yellow-and-green jersey with the number zero proudly displayed. Each jersey had the name Santino on the back.

Twister, who'd been lounging on the porch, bounded out to greet Marianna, whining, his hind end giving credence to his name. Marianna laughed and scratched his ears.

Gina had the ball. Catherina ducked around Alonso, and another sister who looked exactly like Marianna shoved her younger brother out of the way—a definite flag-on-the-play kind of shove—and raced for Gina.

"I forgot." Marianna had a confused expression Ethan had never seen on her face before.

"Forgot what?"

"That this afternoon was our annual Santino football game. Even Gina came back. And I forgot."

Marianna's father, ensconced comfortably in a rocker with a footrest, waved to them from the porch and signed, "Did you get my text?"

Marianna fumbled with her BlackBerry and groaned. "I

felt it go off when I was talking with Misty, then forgot to check it when we left." She read it aloud, "You ok? We're all here. Ready for some football?"

"Sorry, Dad," she called. "Alissa!"

The twin turned, screeched and flew across the yard to envelop her sister in a hug. Again, envy twinged Ethan's emotions at the tight family bond these people shared, but he refused to let it take hold. But he wished. How he wished...

Ethan's father had called and left him a message the night before last, asking for a return phone call. Ethan had honestly meant to do the courteous thing and call back, but in all the craziness, he'd put if off. He fingered his phone and looked for a secluded area. Maybe he could just slip away.

But the moment was lost when the sisters separated and two little girls burst from the house, followed by a blond-headed giant. When the girls saw Marianna, more screeching ensued, and Ethan had a hard time containing his laughter. Their joy was infectious. With the two bundles claiming ownership to her legs, Marianna turned to introduce everyone. She signed as she spoke. "Ready? This is my sister Alissa, her husband, Matthew, and their two precious leeches, Addy and Amy. Addy is six and Amy is three."

Handshakes all around had Ethan's arm hurting and his head pounding to remember all the names.

"I'll get Alonso," she said.

Before Ethan could suggest she let him finish the game, she untangled herself from her nieces and made her way over to her brother, signing something he couldn't see.

Alonso nodded and followed his sister from the game, promising to be right back. Ethan let Marianna guide the three of them over to the side of the yard and under one of the oak trees that offered a bit of privacy. But before she could sign anything, Ethan said, "Let's move into the garage." It wasn't the most protected environment, but it was certainly better than the tree she'd picked. She frowned at him and he explained, "Until I'm sure this is over, I think it's best that you stay within walls and away from windows."

Understanding dawned, and she moved into the spacious garage attached to the house. She then signed to Alonso, "Ethan has some pictures he wants you to look at. Will you see if you can pick out the man who paid you to vandalize my car?"

Her brother winced at the memory, but said, "Sure."

Ethan produced the images and Alonso studied them, his brow furrowed, left hand rubbing the stubble on his young chin. Just as Ethan was ready to jump out of his skin with impatience, Alonso pointed to the picture of Gerald Chambers. "That could be him. But it was so dark, barely any light to even read the notes we were writing back and forth. He had a flashlight on him but kept shining it in our eyes. I just can't be sure." He shrugged, anxiety in his features. "I'm sorry, I really do want to help."

Marianna gave him a one-armed hug. "It's all right. And I believe you."

Relief flooded him, and in a sudden move that took them by surprise, he grabbed Marianna up in a bear hug, let her go and then trotted back to the game.

Ethan saw the tears on her lashes before she blinked them away. All she said was, "Well."

Monday morning brought cold wind and freezing rain. Marianna shivered as she got ready for school, shaking her head and grumbling about the wishy-washy weather. Beautiful day yesterday, yucky stuff today. But that was February in the southeast. Pulling a heavy coat from the hanger, she looked at it and wondered which sister had left it behind. Then she glanced around the room. In spite of the circumstances, she had to admit it had been nice staying here again, allowing her to reminisce about her childhood and teen years.

Blessed didn't begin to describe it. She knew she could never thank God enough for the richness of her life. But it looked as though it would be time to move back into the house she'd shared with Suzanne. Just the thought sent shivers dancing along her nerves.

And she knew she'd never move back there.

Just like that, the decision was made. She'd give her landlord the required thirty days notice and begin house hunting. Until then…

Marianna grabbed a bagel on the way out, opened the door and pulled up short. "Ethan, what are you doing here?"

He sat on the front porch, occupying the rocker her father had only yesterday watched the football game from. Ethan rose and held out a hand. "I'm your escort to and from work until I'm comfortable that this case is closed. Gerald Chambers still isn't talking, and I really think he was working with someone, someone who was pulling his strings. There's just no motive for anything he's done. His actions don't add up."

Warmth tickled her insides as she let him hold the passenger door open for her. He cared. The door shut, she buckled up. Ethan slid in beside her and cranked the car. Marianna said, "Do you think he was the one who attacked me in the gym?"

"I don't know. I'm guessing no."

"Why do you say that?"

"I never smelled cigarettes on him and he never once asked for a smoke during the time we spent together."

Marianna raised a brow. "So, he might have been there to be the decoy?"

"Or simply the lookout. If he saw anyone around, he would cause a distraction."

"Like the vandalism of my car," she muttered.

"He probably had it all planned out if he ran into anyone who questioned him being there. I do think Alonso showing up there was pure coincidence."

Ethan turned left onto Route 56 and headed for the school. "I've got a question for you."

Tilting her head, she shot him a smile. "Sure, what is it?"

"I've been thinking about something. Yesterday, in that alley, that cop yelled at you and you couldn't hear him."

Marianna frowned. "Yes." Where was he going with this?

"Do you ever worry about…"

"What are trying to say, Ethan?" She ignored the familiar scenery zipping by.

"Well, what I mean is, have you ever thought about getting one of those cochlear implant things?"

The crushing devastation that she felt nearly sent her to the floorboard. She stared at him, unable to think, the question echoing through her mind. And then she could only remember Curt's pushing and pushing and then his hand gripping her forearms, fingers squeezing, leaving her with bruises that eventually faded but the final words that never had— "Get a cochlear implant. It's the solution to your problem. Why won't you listen to me? Do as I ask? If you loved me, you'd do it." Then he'd shoved her. Hard.

She'd walked out and never once looked back. And when he'd apologized for his rash behavior, she'd accepted his apology—but moved on without him, recognizing his potential for violence. If he'd kept his hands off her, they might have been able to work through the suddenly obvious issues he had with her hearing impairment, but the combination of the physical abuse and the veiled ultimatum had sent her running. Fast.

Now, as she looked at Ethan, whom she realized had just parked in front of her building, she found she couldn't form an answer to his out-of-the-blue question.

He reached over, took her hand and continued to look at her. Waiting.

Drawing in a deep breath, she shook her head and blew it out, pulling her hand away. "I can't believe you want to change me, too. I thought you were different. I thought I could trust you. I…" She broke off before the tears could fall, stumbling from the car and up the steps to the door.

He probably called her name, but she didn't bother looking back, feeling as though she'd been blindsided, her trust and belief in a future with Ethan shattered into a million little pieces. Marianna stopped at the door, and paused to collect herself. Don't think, don't feel. Get through the day, then get home.

With heart still pounding, her emotions still haywire on the inside, she prayed that at least on the outside she looked normal. A shaking hand opened the door, and she walked slowly toward her classroom. Students began to enter, filtering around her as they went to their lockers. She turned into her room, still feeling zombielike and trying desperately to paste a smile on a face that felt frozen.

Dawn sat at her desk, talking to Victoria, one of the students who'd arrived early to help tutor. The television showed the latest in political news. Slowly, her brain climbed out of the shocked fog, and she began to assimilate the activity around her. Dawn stood and waved, saying, "Since you're here, I'll go run these copies." She grabbed several papers, popped out the door and headed down the hall.

Marianna blinked again, giving an absentminded, belated nod to her disappearing assistant. It was Monday and was supposed to be a day off, a built-in snow day, but since it had snowed right after Christmas break, they'd missed two days. Today was a make-up day. She'd have the older students in her class this morning to help tutor. On Monday, as part of a work program, she had two students, who were interested in the teaching profession, come to her class to help with the kids. Relief made its way through her, and she realized today could be an easy day—if she allowed it. She could sit back and process what had just happened with Ethan.

Then the lights started flashing, the alarm sounded and Marianna groaned in frustration. Why of all days did the administration pick today to run an intruder alert drill? They weren't even supposed to *be* here, for goodness' sake.

A few more students filtered in, and Marianna rushed to

the door to begin the lockdown procedures she and the students had practiced only a month ago.

But when she reached the door, terror hit her as she caught a glimpse of a man in a mask headed straight for her.

This was no drill.

It was the real thing.

She grabbed the doorknob to pull it shut, but horror flooded her as she realized she wouldn't have time to twist the lock.

His hand landed on the knob opposite hers...and pulled.

Ethan drove blindly through the campus, absentmindedly noting the students walking and talking as they made their way to class, bundled up against the unexpected chill the morning had brought. At least the rain had stopped about the time he'd pulled up to Marianna's building.

Marianna.

He blew out a breath. Boy, had he ever said the wrong thing. Why had his question sparked such a reaction? A cochlear implant could help her hear, know when danger was behind her, hear music, laughter. Why wouldn't she want to do that? But he already knew the answer to those questions, should have thought it through before sticking his foot in his mouth.

She was immersed in the deaf culture. Those things didn't bother her; she didn't feel the lack. Or what he and other hearing people would consider lacking. To her, her life was normal. And he just realized why she'd reacted the way she had. Flashes of her smoothing her hair down over her hearing aids taunted him; her statement to Misty about Curt wanting to change her sounded in his memory.

He'd insulted her, had made her feel as if there was something wrong with her. Just like Curt.

Ethan groaned and slapped his head. *Idiot.*

Ashley would have raked him over the coals for that one. And rightly so. But he hadn't asked as in making the suggestion that she should *get* one. He just wanted to know if she'd ever *thought* about it.

Turning off campus, he headed for his office. He had until about three o'clock to find out if he could get anything else from Gerald Chambers and to see if he could get hold of Mrs. Luck. She still hadn't returned his calls. Then he'd head back this way to see if Marianna would accept his apology and let him drive her home.

His cell phone rang, jarring him. Pulling it from the clip, he checked the caller ID: the Luck residence. He turned his scanner down and flipped his phone up to his ear. "Hello?"

"Mr. O'Hara? This is Joshua's grandfather, Ed Luck. We took Joshua out of town over the weekend and just got your message. What can I do for you?"

"Mr. Luck, thanks so much for calling me back. I just had a question for you. Do you know a man by the name of Gerald Chambers?"

"Well, sure, his daddy and Roland were big buddies. Served in the army together and even served on some political committees together."

Nothing he didn't already know. "Is there anything else you can tell me about why Roland came home just before he died? Your wife said his visit was unusual because it was during the week."

"I can't recall anything else. Something seemed to be bothering him, and he spent an awful lot of time in Josh's room. I guess he was missing the boy, or maybe he was feeling guilty sending him to the deaf school so far away. He often said that he should have sent him to some private facility, but what a lot of people don't know is that Roland was a gambler. And while he may have a pretty well-paying job, he had a hard time keeping money in the bank. He couldn't afford a private facility."

That was news. A gambler. Now he might be on to something.

Mr. Luck continued. "I had the impression that he was

looking for something and couldn't find it. I'm sorry I can't be of more help."

"No, no, I appreciate your time." The approaching flashing lights caught Ethan's attention. Several police cars whipped by. Then an ambulance. His pager went off. "Listen, Mr. Luck, if you think of anything else, will you give me a call back?"

"Sure thing, son."

Ethan disconnected the call, then looked at the number on his pager. His boss. He pushed the speed dial button and waited.

Without preamble, the man demanded, "That you, Ethan?"

"Yep. What you got?"

"Another hostage situation, and I need you to make sure things turn out right. I'm sending Dallas as your secondary. I'm coming in, too, as commander."

Dread crawled up him. "Can't Mike Umburger handle it?"

"Nope, he's on medical leave as of yesterday."

Great. "Yes, sir, I'll meet you there. Where?"

"The Palmetto Deaf School. Some lunatic's taken a teacher and some students hostage."

He did a one-eighty, praying he'd be there in time. Dread left him. Sheer nauseating terror took its place.

Marianna hovered near her desk, signing for the students to stay calm, watching the intruder's every move, desperately fighting her own escalating horror. Effortlessly, he'd yanked the door from her hand, stormed in and shoved her back against the whiteboard, bruising her shoulder in the process. He had pulled the door shut behind him.

Then locked it.

The ski mask covered his face. Intense blue eyes peered at her from the slits, his nose covered, his mouth a mere outline under the cloth. She watched the outline move. Shaking, she backed up. Knowing her voice wobbled, she told him, "I know you're saying something, but if I can't see your mouth, I can't read your lips."

He made a motion with a gloved hand—the universal sign for scissors. Marianna swung around and got a pair from her desk. What did he want to use them for? A weapon?

But he already had a gun.

Motioning for her to back up, he grabbed the mask, stuck the scissors in the material where his mouth was and started cutting, making an opening and snipping out a large portion that revealed the lower part of his face, which consisted of firm lips and a strong, freshly shaven jaw.

"Wh-what do you want?"

Still not speaking, he tucked the cutaway cloth into his back pocket and jammed the scissors into the potted plant soil behind him.

Oh, dear Lord, please help us.

Thus far, the man hadn't said a word, at least not one that she'd heard or been able to read; he had merely gestured with the gun. Absentmindedly, her senses took in the details. He was tall, at least a little over six feet. Broad shoulders indicated strength she wouldn't want to test. And his scent tickled her nose. Chewing tobacco. It was the same smell she'd noticed the night she'd been attacked in the gym. Along with the odor of cigarettes.

Cold certainty hit her. This was her attacker, the one who'd left the note in her hand telling her he'd be back. He'd picked her. Her classroom. Her school. He'd come here and put all these people in danger. *She'd* put them in danger. Feeling ill, she turned and looked at her beloved students. Fortunately, two of her students were absent today, so she had three regulars and two deaf student tutors.

Josh stared at the man, his features twisted in confusion. Victoria, one of the deaf students who'd come to help tutor, had fear and revulsion emanating from her as she cowered against the bookshelf behind her. But anger, too, glittered in her eyes. Marianna shot her a look that said, "Don't do anything stupid."

Peter had his forehead touching his desk, his hands wrapped around his head, rocking slowly back and forth. Marianna moved toward him, wanting to offer comfort. The man swung the gun on her. She gasped, backed up, holding her hands up in the universal gesture for surrender.

"What do you want?" she asked him.

Ignoring her, yet keeping the weapon trained on her and the class, he moved to the front of the room. Stepped behind her desk. In a smooth move, he swept the top clean. Marianna flinched. Her purse went sliding, items clattering across the floor.

Next, he pulled the drawers from her desk, rummaging through them then tossing them haphazardly. Still not saying a word.

Glancing around at her terrified students, she signed, "It'll be okay. Just stay calm."

The gun touched her cheek. She froze. Smelled the stale cigarettes again. Turned slowly to see his dark glare. Then he spoke the first words since he'd burst into her classroom. "Don't sign. Understand?"

Marianna nodded, her eyes never leaving his. The eyes of a killer—with a hint of desperation lurking in their depths. She whispered, "Please tell me what you want and I'll give it to you. Anything."

"Sit over there." He gave her a rough shove toward one of the empty student desks. She stepped on an item from her purse, stumbled, grabbed the edge of the chair and sat. He held a hand to his head, looked back at Marianna. "Why is everyone here? No one was supposed to be here."

"Make-up day. It snowed after Christmas so we had to come today."

He kicked a desk and cursed. Then pulled something out of his pocket.

A small plastic bottle full of liquid with wires attaching it to a...cell phone?

Marianna flinched. A bomb of some sort. She'd never seen one before, but she had watched the news, read books, watched crime shows. She looked around, seeing the students' fear, their horror at the turn their lives had just taken.

Victoria had her arms around Christopher, comforting, patting, her angry gaze never leaving the gunman. Marianna vowed to keep an eye on the hotheaded teen. She tried to communicate with her eyes for Victoria to be still, stay calm. The girl shifted, stuck a hand into her coat pocket. Met Marianna's gaze.

Marianna lifted a brow in a silent question. Victoria pulled her hand back out of her pocket and put her arms back around Christopher, her hands strategically placed, with her right hand covering her left. Marianna caught the sign Victoria subtly sent her. If the man had been watching, he'd have thought Victoria was just shifting her hands, but Marianna knew better.

One word. *Sidekick.*

Oh help. The girl had her Sidekick and could use it practically blindfolded.

Did she dare give Victoria the go-ahead to text a message? But Marianna would have to sign the number to her and pray the girl could enter it in without looking at the screen. Or she could call 911. But she couldn't text 911. Could she?

No, she'd call Ethan to be safe. She gave a small negative shake of her head. Victoria's lips thinned. Under the desk, out of sight of the gunman, who was opening every drawer he could find and dumping the contents onto the floor, she signed, "Wait."

The girl nodded, clearly unhappy at the delay, but at least she obeyed.

Marianna's attention was drawn back to the man who suddenly turned and kicked another unoccupied desk, sending it crashing into the wall. She flinched; Victoria jerked and let out a squeal Marianna couldn't hear but could see escape the girl's lips.

The masked intruder turned back to Marianna, gun waving wildly. "Where is it?" He put the gun to poor Josh's head. "Tell me where it is or I'll blow his brains out."

SIXTEEN

Ethan couldn't get to the school fast enough, his brain snapping with the facts. He had to shove aside the terror he felt because in his gut he knew it was Marianna in danger. She and her students.

Someone had had the gall to enter a building on a busy Monday morning and take a class hostage. Chilled, he tried to analyze what that person must be thinking and feeling.

Someone with nothing to lose. And everything to gain by such a rash act. Desperation shouted. And desperation could lead to deadly action.

Which meant he might never get to tell Marianna he was sorry for asking that stupid question about a cochlear implant; he might not get to hold her in his arms. Never kiss her again. *Please, God...*

Unable to form even the simplest prayer, he just let the Holy Spirit intercede on his behalf. God knew. And God was listening. Shocked, Ethan realized he'd wondered ever since Ashley's death if God really did listen. He'd never had the conscious thought that God was ignoring him, but a smack in the face of self-realization had him newly aware that he'd subconsciously stopped thinking of God as One who hears.

Now, he wanted to know God was listening, that God heard his frantic prayers for Marianna and the other innocents who were being threatened by this madman.

Please, God...

But better than anyone, Ethan knew that sometimes bad things happened. God allowed innocent people to be hurt. *Please, let this outcome be different.*

Then he was turning back into the school parking lot, his alarm blaring, the lights swirling on the dash. The campus was on lockdown, the entrances barricaded. The main security guard had been replaced by a local police officer, who let Ethan in the minute she saw him heading toward her.

Ethan whipped past the small building; the vast emptiness of the campus and the unnatural stillness during a normally active school day hit him hard. *Lord, it's not right. There should be kids running around here. Please, please protect them.*

Pulling around to Marianna's building, he swung in behind the authorities already there. Along with campus security. He looked around for the person in charge, the one who would be acting as field commander. The police chief had also just arrived and was barking orders into his phone. When he saw Ethan, he motioned him over.

"What do we got?" He tried to stay professional, refusing to let his fear for Marianna and the kids show through.

"The school's on lockdown. Everyone's got their classrooms shut up. He's confined to one room, so unless the guy starts blazing bullets down the hall and into doors, all but the ones in the room with him should be all right for now. We've got guys working their way into the building. They'll try to set up a surveillance system. I want to keep this contained. We've got the outer perimeter established. Now I want the inside done."

"What room is he in?" He already knew the answer, but couldn't quite help the wave of nausea that swept him when the man pointed to Marianna's window. "That one. We've got a sniper on the roof of the building over there." He gestured behind him. "Guy can see right in, but the teacher's in the way. He's got her sitting in a seat in front of the window. Unfortunately, he's smart."

"Let's pray we're smarter. Has contact been established?"

"Nope. There's no phone in the room. We've got a throw phone but nowhere to throw it." Often when a phone wasn't available in a situation like this, one of the SWAT members would toss a phone to the hostage taker. "I got the teacher's cell number, but she's deaf and hasn't answered it. No answer to my texts either."

But she was alive. He could see her sitting there in plain view, her back to him. Next to her was a male student, probably one of her tutors who came in to help first thing in the morning. The guy may be smart, but he wasn't thinking. He hadn't pulled the blinds yet. "How many in the classroom?"

This wasn't a planned situation. Which meant the guy was trying to think as he went.

"She's got two absent. There are four males and one female student. And the teacher. Marianna Santino."

"All right. We need contact. Also get me the blueprints for this building. I want a microphone and camera in there somehow."

"The boys are working on it. Here's your mic—it's rigged and ready. You say the word and the boys will storm the door. You're the boss here, Ethan. This is what you've been trained for." The man clapped him on the back. "You'll be fine."

So, he hadn't done a very good job of hiding his nerves. Now wasn't the time to think about failure. Failure meant someone would die. And if that happened, they might as well go ahead and dig his grave as well.

Marianna had thrown herself at Josh, wrapping her arms around the boy, who didn't really have a clue he was in danger, and defiantly stared down the man with the gun. She could only pray he couldn't see the sick fear that had her trembling.

His anger was escalating. Not finding what he wanted, he

was losing control. But he wouldn't tell her what he was looking for. Every drawer had been pulled out and overturned. Finally, he'd snorted in disgust and moved the gun from Josh.

He was now working on the shelves, pulling stuff off, opening every container, every educational game; he missed nothing. And each time he didn't find what he wanted, he destroyed something else.

And the TV played on above Marianna, creating normalcy where none existed. She wondered if the authorities would soon cut the power. Until then, a commercial depicting Pampers ended and a shot of the two political candidates debating issues flashed. Campaign headquarters celebrated victories. Normal life.

God, please get us back to normal. Safe and normal. But Marianna knew she'd never be the same again.

She shot a glance at Victoria. The girl had sneaked her hand back in her pocket, just waiting for the signal. Marianna gave it to her. While the gunman's back faced her, she quickly signed the first three digits of Ethan's phone number. Victoria moved only a fraction. Marianna blinked—no wonder she'd never caught the girl texting in class. Watching the man move to the next shelf, she waited as he whirled, looked at her, the other students acting like statues, then he went back to his search.

The next four numbers flew from her fingers and Victoria nodded. The number was in. Now for the message:

ONE MAN. MASK. ONE GUN. 9 MM. ONE BOMB. VERY MAD. LOOKING FOR SOMETHING. HE CAN'T FIND IT. HELP PLEASE.

Again, Victoria moved almost imperceptibly, her features paling at the word *bomb*, but didn't stop typing with one hand.

All of a sudden, the man turned toward the window. Victoria froze. He stomped to the window and shoved it open a fraction and listened; then Marianna saw him swear. He turned to her and held out his hand. "Cell phone."

She watched his lips move, but it took a moment for the two words to process. Grabbing her by the arm, he yanked her up, shoving his face closer to hers. "Give. Me. Your. Cell. Phone."

She pulled away. "It...fell on the floor, under my desk when you..." She made the sweeping motion he'd done earlier.

"Get it."

Bending down, she spotted the device—and her can of Mace sitting right beside it.

Ethan held the department cell phone and let Marianna's phone ring, not letting himself think about what he would do if the man refused to talk. Each incident had a personality all its own. There were no absolutes in crisis negotiation. *Help me, God.*

He felt a hand on his shoulder and turned to find Dallas Montgomery standing there. Relief shuddered through him. Backup. Another trained hostage negotiator who could be his secondary, help him out if he needed it.

The phone still rang. Soon it would trip to voice mail. Then he saw Marianna pulled away from the window. His heart nearly stopped when she disappeared from view. Part of him waited for the sound of the gunshot. He was almost surprised when a voice barked in his ear. "What?"

Ethan's personal cell buzzed on his hip. He ignored it. "Hey, man. My name's Ethan and I'm with the police force here. I've been called in to help with this situation, to see that we can resolve it without anyone getting hurt. Can you help me out?"

Establish contact, offer assistance. The basics of crisis negotiation training.

The phone clicked off.

Ethan growled in frustration. If the man wouldn't talk, Ethan couldn't do his job. And the tactical team made up of SWAT members would have to move in. Which meant

Marianna and everyone in the building would be in extreme danger.

One thing Ethan knew he had on his side was time. As long as no one was getting hurt, things could end peacefully.

"Call him back." Dallas started setting up behind him. He'd keep track of the conversation—assuming one happened—and any details he could pick up, offering advice to Ethan as he handled the man.

Dialing the number, Ethan prayed for the man to pick up again. It kept ringing. Then Marianna appeared back in the window, seated once again.

The phone finally clicked. "I'm not talking. Don't call back."

"Wait!"

A sigh. "I'm rather busy. Not in the mood for a chat. *Ciao.*"

Click.

Restraining the desire to hurl the phone to the asphalt below, Ethan gripped it until his knuckles turned white.

Dallas shook his head. The big Texan had worry stamped all over his features. "Nothing you can do if he won't talk, Ethan."

Think, think, Ethan.

"He's educated. Cultured."

Dallas nodded. *"Ciao?"*

Ethan's personal phone vibrated that he had a message. Rubbing his forehead, he paced. At the next vibration he snapped the phone out of its case and almost tossed it. Instead, something made him click to see who the message was from.

He didn't recognize the number, but he pressed the button to read it anyway, his mind not on the device in his hands but on how to get the man on the phone and keep him there.

Then the message caught his full attention. And sent fear shuddering through him.

A message from Marianna. Somehow, she'd managed to

text him. Probably from a student's phone. He didn't bother questioning how—he was just grateful. But if he responded, would the thing make a noise? He couldn't take a chance, could only hope for periodic updates.

He turned back to Dallas and waved his phone. "I've got contact. One of the students managed a text."

Alarm made Dallas's eyes go wide. "Oh, man, I hope he doesn't catch on to that."

"Yeah. He's got a bomb. We need a bomb squad ASAP."

Dallas immediately got on the radio, calling for the evacuation of the team that had entered the building. They would let the SWAT team go in and remove as many of the hostages that they could reach without the gunman knowing they were in there.

What was this guy thinking? What was he doing? What did he want?

And why wouldn't he talk?

Josh had pushed Marianna away, so she slipped back into her seat, thinking, taking in every detail she could process. She stared at the television. Desperately thinking, praying.

Her cell phone must have rung again, because the gunman pulled it up and pushed a button. Refusing to talk again, Marianna feared. Then he was in her face once again. "Where's that box you keep for that kid Josh?"

"What?"

He gave her a shake and her neck whiplashed back, then forward. She winced. Wanting to shut her eyes and turn from the foul breath on her face, she instead forced herself to watch his lips carefully. "Pay close attention, teacher. Where's the box?"

"That box? This is about that *box?* I don't have it." There was no way she was going to tell him that box was just down the hall in another teacher's classroom. Where another teacher had a roomful of students.

A scream of frustration erupted from him, and Marianna

cringed, this time unable to keep her eyes trained on him. He shoved her aside once more, and she fell on the heating/air-conditioning unit under the window. When she looked out, she had the view she'd seen thousands of times over the last few years. Only this time, the entire front part of the building was cordoned off, emergency vehicles surrounding it.

She thought she saw a news camera, various staff members being held back.

And Ethan standing behind a police car was looking up with an expression she'd never seen on his face before.

Sheer terror.

Ethan pushed the raging fear down. Shoved aside the visions of the gun going off and Marianna…

No, he had to focus, to do his job. Pray as if he'd never prayed before. She'd appeared for an instant. He'd seen her come flying against the window. She must have made the guy mad, and if he refused to answer the cell one more time, things were going to have to change. His commander would pull rank and force an entrance.

Ethan didn't want to see that. There had to be a better way. Dallas clapped his shoulder, pulled the blueprints over and pointed out entry points. Kevin, head of campus security, came over. "Can I help in any way?"

Dallas showed him the blueprints. "We've got guys stationed here and here with rifles ready to take him out as soon as we get the word, but he's staying out of the line of fire. As long as everyone else stays in their classrooms, they should be fine. There's no way for him to enter the way they're set up. Our problem is getting into the room this guy's in. Only one entryway. A very small window opening. Not advantageous for us, for sure."

"You'll have to wait him out." Kevin shook his head.

"And we can't get the camera in because of the bomb threat." Ethan said.

"Bomb squad's on the way. SWAT team just arrived."

Ethan rubbed a hand over his jaw and glanced back up at the window, pulled out the official cell and dialed Marianna's number again.

Marianna watched the intruder alternate between swearing and pacing. Then he pulled her phone from his pocket and slapped it to his ear. "Not talking." He hung up and looked at Marianna. "You're lying."

She swallowed hard. *Lord, Jesus, what do I do?*

Slowly, with even, measured steps, he walked over to stand in front of her. "You're lying, and if you don't start talking, I'm going to start shooting." He moved the gun around, "Now, who do you want to be first?"

Victoria cringed. Marianna wanted to scream. Josh just watched with a confused expression on his face. Peter still had his head down, and Christopher kept his face buried in Victoria's arms.

Marianna lifted her chin. "I might have an idea where it could possibly be. If you'll let them go, I'll tell you."

He laughed. "You're not in a bargaining position."

"But we have to move. If you would just let them go and keep me, it'll be a lot simpler."

He studied her, then cursed when the phone rang again. But he picked it up, and listened and then said, "Yeah, I want something. I want a million bucks and to live in the Hamptons, but it's not happening right now."

A pause.

"I tell you what—I'll let all the kids go. Every last one of them. Get everyone out of the building. Except this room."

Another pause.

"I don't care about those kids. I don't want to hurt them. I just need—" he snapped his mouth shut, then continued "—get 'em out, but if I see one uniform in here, I'll start sending out bodies—or just blow the place up."

Hope blossomed in her chest. Why the sudden turnabout? Had she managed to convince him? She looked over at

Victoria to see if the girl had caught any of the conversation. She had her eyes on Marianna. Marianna gave her a slight shrug and shook her head. No more texting. Not yet.

What did he need with Josh's box? And how did he even know about it? What had Josh put in there that would cause someone to take an entire building hostage?

Ten minutes later, to her relief, through the slim side window next to her door, Marianna could see the students and teachers filing past. The gunman simply watched the commotion from his perch on her stool, his little bomb sitting on the smaller desk situated in front of the whiteboard.

Victoria shifted restlessly. Peter still had his head down, refusing to look up. Marianna worried about the long-term effects this would have on him. He was such a sensitive boy. But she couldn't think about that now. She had to stay calm and cool, think about what she could do to help the authorities get them out of this.

The gunman stood. She tensed. He moved the pistol her way. She flinched. "Now it's our turn. Get those kids out of here."

Ethan watched the steady stream of students and staff flow from the building and be pulled behind the police line into the safe zone. The SWAT team kept it efficient as several others entered the building and swept the rooms they could get to without being seen from the gunman's room. As the newly released hostages entered the zone, officers patted down each person and checked IDs. Couldn't be too careful. The principal had been called up to identify each and every person exiting the building as an added precaution.

Two students followed who made Ethan's breath hitch in his throat. He recognized them as students from Marianna's classroom. He spoke into his radio. "Hey, what's the classroom looking like?"

"He had the teacher pull the blinds."

Ethan sent up a swift prayer. Every hostage situation had its own dynamics, but this...this one was driving him nuts; it was so totally off the charts in the crisis negotiation arena. The process wasn't working; following procedure was netting him zilch. He was going to have to go with his gut.

"Chief, I suggest sending the bomb squad in there. I only received one text message, and the guy won't stay on the phone. This feels...weird. This isn't a normal hostage situation. Something tells me this guy hadn't planned on a bunch of people being here today." He shook his head, praying he was making the right decision. He looked his chief in the eye. "Send the team in. Now."

The man stared at Ethan for a brief moment, searching for something and seeming to find it. He nodded and trotted off. Ethan spun on his heel and approached the student he thought was named Peter and signed, "Can you tell me anything about Marianna?"

The boy covered his head and shook. Ethan backed away, sorrow filling him. How had these kids lives been changed? How much damage would this do to them? Fury filled him and he vowed to get this guy.

A hand touched his arm. A dark-headed girl signed, "I'm Victoria. I was in the classroom with Ms. Santino. She told the man she'd show him where something he was looking for was. And she'd show him how to get out of the building if he'd let us go. He did, and I saw him pull her out of the classroom."

Ethan's earpiece crackled; then a voice said, "Classroom is empty. Bomb squad's working on the bomb. Guy's got the teacher and is on the run!"

Ethan swung back toward the girl. "Do you know where she would take him?"

Victoria shrugged, worry pulling her brows toward the bridge of her nose. "No. There's no way out except this door and the one on the other end. Oh, and the one door upstairs."

Ethan envisioned where he had men stationed. All those

doors were covered. If the guy so much as stuck his head out, a sniper would put a bullet in it.

He looked around, then back at the building. All students and staff were accounted for—except Marianna and the gunman.

Marianna stumbled along after her captor. She debated taking him down to Cleo's classroom but knew as soon as she gave him what he wanted, she was dead.

Quickly, she'd said, "I don't have what you're looking for. But I might be able to help you find it. There are a couple of places it could be."

"Shut up," he'd snarled. But Marianna persisted.

"I'll help you search the entire building, plus I know another way out, a way past the police. I promise." Another question struck her. Why did he have a bomb with him if he'd thought the building would be empty?

Cold chills broke out over her flesh as she answered her own question. Because if he didn't find what he was looking for, he would blow the place up and leave absolutely no trace of it, just in case it *was* here and he didn't find it. Which meant he couldn't take a chance on someone seeing it.

"I don't have time to search this building. As soon as they realize we're not in that classroom, they're going to swarm this place." His gaze narrowed, "Now find it so I can get out of here."

Her heart fluttered in fear. She started to speak when he flinched. She wondered what he had heard. He grabbed her arm. "Someone's coming." He pulled her around, his blue eyes glittering down into hers, his mouth tight as he demanded, "Get me out of here or I'll blow you away right now...and anyone else I come across, got it?"

"Yes." She shook. He was serious. He wouldn't have any reservations about shooting her. But he needed her right now. She took a deep breath. "Follow me."

"What a waste of..." he muttered. "I can't believe this

has…all this trouble for a stupid box that's possibly not even here."

Marianna watched his face, his lips move, the shape of his jaw, the outline of his lips, the slight tilt to his head. And blinked. Could it be? No, no way.

But she knew it was. A deaf person was very aware of body language, and his just shouted his identity.

Shock and disbelief racked her.

She knew him. Knew who this man holding the gun was. Her mind sputtered, stalled. How? Why?

Her danger meter just rang off the charts. If caught, this man had a lot to lose. And Marianna knew he had no intention of being caught.

And if he realized she knew his identity, she was as good as dead.

Against his boss's wishes, Ethan ran into the building, ordering, "Don't come after me until I call for help. If we all descend on him, he'll kill her."

"Ethan, you're going to get yourself killed." Victor's voice came through loud and clear, but Ethan's focus was on Marianna's safety, not his own. He darted down to the classroom and screeched to a halt. Empty. Just as he'd been told. Where would they go? The roof?

No. As clear as if Marianna had whispered it in his ear, he knew.

The basement.

But no exit door had been shown on the blueprints. He'd specifically looked to see if he needed coverage on one. Why would she go down there? She'd have no way of getting out. Cold terror swept his insides. Marianna was sacrificing herself for her students.

Probably trying to buy some time. Did she have a plan? Did she think she could get away from the guy while down in the basement? Or did she know something he didn't?

Spinning from the door, Ethan headed for the steps that

would lead him down. With fingers wrapped around his gun, he kept his focus, his senses tuned to the atmosphere around him.

I'm coming, Marianna, I'm coming.

Marianna felt her ankle twist in the dimly lit area as she maneuvered over and around the accumulation of *stuff*. The basement held tons of storage from years past. File cabinets littered the area along with boxes of long forgotten books, paper, files. A path had been cut through the mess, and she knew this was because maintenance workers had to get down here occasionally to work. Or flip a switch in the breaker box. Her left hand caught on a stack of files, sending them to the floor.

Her captor didn't stop, just tugged her along. She had to figure out a way to get away from the man, who kept a tight grip on her upper right arm. If she could get free and could get to the Mace she had in her front right pocket…

But he hadn't let go of her arm.

Please, Jesus, help me. Let me have a clear mind, be smart. Think, Marianna. Look around you. Get away from him.

But there was no way. He yanked her around to face him. "Show me. I need out of here, now. There's no way I'm getting caught, you understand?"

She nodded, her brain humming. He just needed to let go of her. And if she couldn't get to the little canister in her pocket, she needed some other kind of weapon. Meeting his eyes, she shivered at the coldness there. Death stared back at her.

Swallowing hard, she pointed to the back. He pushed her on, over to the window with the broken latch. She had discovered it just a couple of weeks ago when she'd followed a stray cat who'd recently given birth. The cat had slipped inside, and Marianna knew she had kittens she was taking care of.

She'd planned to report it to the maintenance department but had wanted to give the kittens time to grow a bit before they were forced from their home. Now, perhaps her compassionate nature might be the deciding factor in whether this man let her go or shot her.

Depending on if he thought he could fit through the window.

Marianna doubted he could fit but hoped he would try. Maybe it would give her a chance to run, since she feared he would not let her go once he had his escape down. She shuddered. As soon as he was distracted, she needed to be able to act immediately, needed to be quick and smart.

Please give me an opening, just a chance to get away.

She was going to use the fact that she knew the layout of the basement much better than he. If she could just get out of his sight, she might have a chance. But as long as he kept a hand clamped on her arm, she wasn't going anywhere.

Her eyes darted. The lighting was poor, but maybe that could work to her advantage also.

If she could get away, she could hide somewhere— behind the massive number of bookshelves, a filing cabinet; anything would do.

When he shoved her in front of him, she stumbled, her knee banging the side of a file cabinet. Pain shot up her leg, but she ignored it. That was minor when compared with the bullet she felt quite sure was waiting for her as soon as he decided he didn't need her anymore.

"Here." She pointed to the window that sat at face level. He pulled her back, moved her to his right side and gripped her upper left arm with his right hand this time. With the gun, he reached up and shoved the window open. It slapped back down, and he turned back to Marianna.

The voice growled, "Sit there." His lips curved into a cruel smile as he shoved her onto a sturdy wooden crate.

She sat.

Breathing a prayer of thanks, she shoved her right hand into her front pocket. Fingers curled around the can of Mace just as he swung the gun around to aim it point-blank at her heart.

* * *

Ethan stepped lightly down the steps, his gun gripped tight in his right hand, his eyes finally adjusting to the darker environment. He heard scrapes, a thud, come from up ahead. The radio crackled in his ear, but he didn't dare answer. Right now, he figured the guy probably thought no one knew where he was. And he sure didn't want to tip off the attacker to the contrary. He kept his breathing shallow, ignored the adrenaline infusing him.

Move slow; move smart. Don't dwell on the fear that if you fail, she'll die.

He couldn't stop the mental picture of him screaming, of Ashley never knowing he called her name, of Ashley being hit by the car, flying through the air. His feelings of helplessness, horror, the crippling guilt that he couldn't protect her.

But now Marianna needed him. He breathed deeply. He ordered himself, to focus, keep it together. *Lord, I need You.*

Three more steps brought him to the bottom of the staircase. Breathing through his nose, he held himself still, tuned his ears to the slightest sound.

Nothing. He kept moving, heard a whisper, felt the chill of musty air brush by like a swish of evil against his face. He shivered, not from the cold but from the oppressiveness he felt. In his mind he quoted every verse he could think of. *I will never leave you nor forsake you. Lo, I am with you always, even unto the end of the earth. Trust in Me. I am the way, the truth and the light.*

Moving forward, he kicked up some papers in the middle of the path. He stepped over them, wishing he could see who he was tracking.

Another slight sound from his left reached his ears, then a single word. "Here." Slowly, he crept forward. One foot after the other until his foot came down on something soft. The yowling screech nearly took his head off, and the bite of sharp claws sank into his left calf.

* * *

Marianna knew if she moved a scant millimeter, the man would pull the trigger. Hardly daring to breathe, she watched his eyes. Knew when he'd made the decision. Knew she was on her way to meet face-to-face the God she loved. His finger curled around the trigger.

Lord, I can't give up without a fight. Please let me live to love Ethan.

Her hand gripped the canister. She refused to sit obediently while he blew her away.

A fleeing ball of fur caught her eye just as his focus swung from her to behind him, his attention diverted, his eyes off her. Marianna dove to the left, pulled the Mace from her pocket and aimed it at his eyes, which were now back on her.

She held her breath and squeezed. Liquid squirted, covering his eyes and his nose, soaking the cloth still covering his face. As though she were in slow motion, she could see his mouth working, could see him stumble away, clawing his face with his free hand. The hand that held the gun jerked toward the ceiling, and she saw the flash of the bullet exiting the barrel.

Then she was back in real time, scrambling from her position on the floor, hurrying away from the man who wanted her dead, her mind looping a prayer: *Please, Jesus, please!*

With her heart thudding painfully in her chest, she moved fast, her elbow catching the edge of something hard, which sent shooting pains into her shoulder. Panting, she followed the trail she'd just walked with the man behind her. Any minute now, she expected to feel a bullet blast into her back. Still, she skirted the debris, maneuvered through file cabinets, boxes. The floor thumped behind her. A bullet pinged from the pole beside her.

She screamed and jerked sideways, tripped and fell.

SEVENTEEN

An agonized cry sounded and chilled Ethan's soul. It echoed madness, fury, murder. Marianna had done something to make the man *very* mad. That was definitely not a good thing. Ethan's heart nearly stopped when he heard the whine and clang of the bullet. Marianna's responding scream froze him for a brief second; then he picked up the pace and headed toward her. He wanted to hurry, to burst on the scene and grab her away.

Still, caution reigned. If he went and got himself shot, he wasn't going to be much help for her. He had to get to her, had to save her. The responsibility weighed heavily on his shoulders as his prayers to God continued.

As he swept the basement with his eyes, his senses, the acid in his stomach churned, ate at him. What if he couldn't save her? What if he failed again? The what-ifs could haunt him.

But God was still in control.

If someone had landed a punch on his jaw, he wouldn't have been more stunned.

It wasn't up to Ethan.

It was up to God.

He swung the gun to the right. Someone still thrashed ahead. Another gunshot, the bullet grazing the ceiling above him. He ducked.

God was in control.

Ethan was only a tool.

Marianna's life was in God's hands. Not Ethan's.

The realization scared him to death...and freed him all at the same time. What if God chose to let Marianna die at the hands of the man who had her, the man who still screamed obscenities and threats?

Please, Lord, use me. I believe prayer changes things. I know You don't need me, but use me to save her.

Closer, closer to the noise. Where are you, Marianna?

A shuffle to his left. He whirled and stared into Marianna's shocked, fear-filled eyes; then something hit him in the left shoulder, spinning him around to crash against a file cabinet. Again, Marianna's scream echoed around him.

He looked down to see a small stain growing larger. Then searing pain hit him. Marianna grabbed his hand and pulled him behind the makeshift wall of shelves where she'd been hiding. Then the shelves parted, crashing to the ground, and the masked gunman stood, his weapon trained on them. Marianna squealed and Ethan thought she sounded more angry than scared.

The man's blue eyes, rimmed in red, ran with tears—and glittered with rage. Ethan held his gun on him. "Drop it," he ordered.

A guttural laugh scraped Ethan's ears. Then to his horror and fury, the man turned his gun on Marianna and said, "*You* drop it."

Cold fear settled in the pit of Ethan's stomach. If he dropped the gun, they were dead. If he took a chance and shot the man, the guy might get a shot off and Marianna would be dead regardless.

Please, Lord, a little help.

Marianna knew Ethan would drop his weapon to save her. She couldn't let that happen. He already looked pale, his breathing coming in shallow spurts, the stain on his shoulder growing by the minute. The gunman stared at her, and she swallowed at the evil emanating from him. She'd really made him angry with the Mace stunt. Terror washed over her, and she considered her options.

"Don't drop that gun, Ethan." She knew her voice shook but didn't care. The look on his face said he felt he had to protect her, that if something happened to her, he'd never live through it. Not after what had happened to Ashley.

"Why?" Ethan's simple question caught the man's attention.

He blinked. "What?"

"Why? What do you want?"

A delaying tactic.

"I don't have time to explain my reasons to you. Now either drop the gun or she dies."

She blurted, "He wants Josh's box."

The man gritted his teeth. "Shut up." His finger tightened on the trigger, then Marianna felt herself flying through the air, heard the crack of a gun. Fear cramped her as she heard another loud pop, then gave a grunt as she landed with a thump in a pile of files.

"Ethan!"

No sooner had his name left her lips than SWAT members and local police flooded the place. The gunman lay face-down, screaming his anger, with cuffs encircling each wrist, a steady flow of blood pumping from his right hand. Ethan sagged against a pole, pale, shaken, with a hand pressed against his left side. Blood seeped between his fingers. Marianna scrambled out of the files, ignoring the cloud of dust that hovered around her and scooted over to Ethan. "Ethan, oh, no. You've been shot again."

He grimaced, reached for her and pulled her down to lay a kiss on her lips. When he moved back, he groaned. "I promised myself I was going to do that if you were all right. Are you all right?"

She nodded, tears clogging her throat.

"Then that's all that matters. I can die a happy man now." He gave her a weak grin and she shuddered.

"What on earth are you talking about?"

"I kissed you again. I can die happy now."

Paramedics began easing him into a horizontal position. Marianna wanted to slug him...and kiss him again. "You'd better not die on me. You've got a lot to live for."

He looked into her eyes, and she could see the emotion behind them. "I'm sorry for what I said in the car...about the cochlear..."

This time it was Marianna who leaned down and kissed him. "Don't worry about it. I was just a little sensitive about the issue."

Her heart hurt at the relief she saw flood his face. Then his eyes turned to the still masked gunman. "Who is he?"

She gave a shudder. "Steven Marshbanks, campaign manager for the man who'll probably be the next governor of South Carolina."

Ethan's eyes went wide; then he passed out.

When Ethan wakened, the first thing he noticed was the ache in his shoulder and the fire in his side. The second thing was the beautiful woman sleeping on the couch beside him. Shifting, he grunted at the shaft of pain, but Marianna didn't stir. The door swooshed open and a woman in a white lab coat entered. "Hello, Mr. O'Hara, and welcome back to consciousness."

The stirring of the air must have swept over Marianna, because her eyes popped open and she sat up. Immediately her gaze darted to Ethan and a warmth he'd never felt before coursed through him as he saw the relief in her eyes that he was safe.

And would live.

She gave him a tentative smile. "I'll wait outside if you like."

The doctor glanced at the chart, then looked at Marianna.

"That's all right. Mr. O'Hara will be staying with us one more night. If all goes well, he'll be released to head home tomorrow. The bullet in his shoulder passed clean through, causing only some minor damage. The bullet in his side just creased it." She gave him a pointed look. "You are one very lucky man."

He looked at Marianna. "The luckiest."

Then the doctor said to Marianna, "He's healing nicely, and as long as he doesn't overdo it, he will be good as new in a couple of months."

The doctor left and Marianna turned to say something to him, but before she had a chance, the door opened and Victor, Ethan's boss, entered. "Ethan, glad to see you awake. I do appreciate you not dying on me as I need some details filled in on this blank report."

A grin stretched across Ethan's lips. "Good to see, you too, Chief. Try to go easy on the sympathy, will you?"

Victor's expression softened for a fraction of a second. "Glad you're all right, man. We let your parents know what happened. They said they'd stop by shortly."

"Thanks." He wondered if they would, though. Not wanting to dwell on that topic, he said, "So, fill us in. What was so important that Steven Marshbanks risked his career, his life and everything he holds dear to get his hands on?"

Victor nodded toward Marianna. "She gave us the box that he seemed to be after. Apparently, Josh snatched a flash drive with a lot of incriminating evidence."

"Really? What was on it?"

"An entire list of campaign contributors, the amounts they gave…and where the funds went, a lot of personal spending, bank account numbers, investments—all kinds of stuff."

"Whoa. Where did the funds go?"

Victor grunted. "A lot of places they shouldn't have. And we played a little game with Gerald Chambers. When we told Gerald we had Steven Marshbanks in custody and the man was casting all the blame on him, the boy sang like Tweety."

"What did Chambers have to do with Marshbanks?"

Victor leaned against the edge of the bed, and Marianna spoke for him. "The three of them were all connected, weren't they? Roland Luck, Gerald Chambers and Steven Marshbanks."

"Yep." Victor nodded and Ethan tried to put it all together, but his brain felt a big foggy. He blamed it on the pain meds, not the woman who'd walked up and taken hold of his hand.

"So?"

"So," Marianna said, thoughtfully, "Roland Luck came across the evidence. As the campaign manager, he would have to keep an accounting of the money, know where it was spent, and so forth."

Victor nodded. "Right. Apparently, he noticed something amiss and did a little digging, trying to figure out what was going on. He copied the stuff to a flash drive and took it home with him on a weekend visit to his parents."

Ethan chimed in. "That must have been what he was looking for when he went by his parents' house in the middle of the week. And when he didn't find it, he realized Josh must have snatched it and taken it to school."

"He actually searched your classroom, Marianna," Victor said, "but you never realized it."

"I knew someone had messed with my desk that morning! It was the week after Suzanne's funeral. I went back to work and my desk had been rearranged…everything was…off."

Ethan's lips tightened at the thought of the invasion of her privacy…her classroom, her home…her life. "When he didn't find it there, he went to your house."

"Suzanne," Marianna said, breathing.

Victor nodded. "That was pure accident, we believe. Roland figured the house would be empty for a while, but Suzanne walked in on him. It scared him. She started screaming at him, she grabbed for the phone to call the police and he shoved her. She fell, hit her head and bled to death."

Tears leaked down Marianna's cheeks. "It's all so needless. If she'd stayed at work, she'd still be alive."

Ethan shook his head and squeezed Marianna's hand. He looked at Victor. "So, I'm guessing it's not a coincidence that Roland Luck died in that car accident."

"Nope. We're pretty sure that was a setup. Failed brakes on a steep, winding mountainous road." He shook his head. "Steven Marshbanks arranged the meeting for the campaign coordinators and volunteers. At the top of the mountain. He cut the brake line. Luck got in the car, started down and ended up over the side. Poor guy never had a chance. He was just trying to figure out where the money was going and who was behind the theft of it. So he broke into Marianna's house to find the drive, caused Suzanne's death—and ended up dead himself for his efforts."

"And Marshbanks is spilling all this?"

Victor shrugged. "Hey, we got him for kidnapping, attempted murder, and every other charge you can possibly think of. I think we can even get him for a terrorist act because of the bomb he brought into the school. Against his lawyer's advice, this guy is talking faster than we can listen, trying to cut a deal."

"Okay, Roland killed Suzanne by accident." Ethan mused. "Then Gerald was the one in Marianna's house that night she called me."

"Yeah, the DNA evidence showed us that, plus, he finally confessed. It seems that Roland was so riddled with guilt about what he'd done to Suzanne that he went back and told Marshbanks all about it, including the fact that Roland suspected Clayton Robertson was helping himself to campaign funds."

Marianna took over, thinking out loud. "But it wasn't Clayton. It was Marshbanks—the very man Roland took into his confidence."

"Which is why Roland ended up dead. Marshbanks realized Roland had the evidence but had lost it, couldn't find it at your house.... So, Marshbanks had to get his hands on that flash drive—and fast."

"Which is why he came after me—or rather, Josh's box. He figured I'd put it where I always did. When I didn't send it home as usual, he came after it. And he probably didn't want to call asking for it because he didn't want to draw attention to it. What if I'd been the kind of person who'd look at it? No, he couldn't risk that." Marianna's shoulders drooped. "But how did Marshbanks and Gerald Chambers get together?"

Victor held up a finger. "That one took a bit of work. Roland Luck, Steven Marshbanks and Chase Chambers, Gerald's father, were all in the army together and big buddies for years. Marshbanks knew he couldn't have too many unexplained absences with all the campaigning going on, so he hired Gerald to do some of his dirty work for him. That kid's been in trouble since he got caught with a knife in elementary school. Marshbanks knew this and was able to talk him into breaking into Marianna's house by promising him big bucks and a huge political future. Gerald was dumb enough to fall for it. If he hadn't been caught, I can guarantee you, Gerald would be dead right now."

"At Steven Marshbanks's hand."

Ethan watched Marianna's brain clicking, absorbing the information. He said, "So when Gerald was arrested and the flash drive was still missing, Steven couldn't take a chance on hiring someone else and had to come and do the dirty work himself."

Marianna shook her head. "Only he never expected to run into a campus full of people. But why not wait? Why take a building full of hostages?"

"Greed," Victor said. "On that flash drive was vital information with a deadline. He had to have it for some investment deal or he would have been out millions of dollars."

"It wasn't on the computer Roland Luck copied it from?"

"Apparently not. I think Roland realized to some extent what was going on and in a fit of pique erased a lot of the information, and Marshbanks didn't know how to get it back.

A computer forensics person probably would know, but he couldn't exactly ask for help on that. So his only hope was that flash drive."

Ethan leaned his head back and closed his eyes. Exhaustion swamped him. He looked back up at his boss. "Thanks, Victor."

Victor clapped him on the shoulder. "You did a good job, Ethan. You called everything just right at the school hostage scene. You should feel proud of yourself."

Emotion clogged his throat. "I'm just glad no one else got hurt."

Victor turned toward the door, saying, "I'll see you when the doctor releases you back to work."

"I'll be back sooner than you think."

"Ha!" Marianna snorted. "I'll add that to my list of things to discuss with you."

Ethan raised a brow, loving the fire that lit her eyes from the inside. "My pleasure, ma'am, my pleasure."

Marianna couldn't believe everything that had happened in the last twenty-four hours. Incredibly, she felt at peace. About everything. Naturally, she felt sorrow at the death of her friend, the trauma her students had suffered and the destructive greed leading people to make decisions that would negatively impact so many lives.

But for her, peace reigned. God was in control. He'd protected her and her students—and used this wonderful man to do so.

"Mom wants you to come to the house when you're released from the hospital."

Ethan kept a grip on her hand, his thumb rubbing back and forth across her knuckles, causing shivers to dance along her nerves. The light in his eyes spoke about feelings he hadn't allowed to cross his lips yet. She kicked herself. Why had she ever compared this man to Curt Wentworth? The two were as different as night and day.

But she'd been so hurt by Curt that she'd allowed it to blind her to Ethan's true motives. Good motives. She'd been looking at him suspiciously because of one warped experience, and she'd been wrong.

He said, "I appreciate that, but I don't want to put her out."

"She'll be put out if you turn her down." She frowned at him. "And then I'll get grilled about why I couldn't talk you into coming. So, plan on it, okay?" He pulled her down to sit on the bed beside him, wincing only a little as the bed shifted. She hurt for him. Marianna bit her lip, fought more tears and said, "You saved my life."

The simple words provoked tears. She watched him look to the ceiling, blink them back. "No, I finally came to the realization that I am powerless...except for the power of God."

"You pushed me out of the path of the gun and got shot. You saved me."

He nodded. "I can't explain to you what I was going through in that basement. The whole time I was looking for you, I felt helpless, yet I was praying."

"And God was listening."

"Yes. He used me to help you, and I feel—" he took a deep breath and let it out "—free, I guess, is the word."

"Ashley's death was a horrible, horrible thing, but it wasn't your fault."

His grip tightened for a brief moment. "You can read me like a book, can't you?"

She looked him in the eye. "I love you, Ethan."

Shock flashed back at her—and something else. Pleasure? She couldn't be sure, but she didn't regret saying the words. He opened his mouth, but she placed a finger over his lips. "Shush. You don't have to say the words back to me. They don't come with a required response. They come from my heart, and I wanted you to know."

Funny, she didn't feel embarrassed that she'd told him, nor self-conscious. Once again, Ethan started to say something, then snapped his mouth shut and turned his attention to the door. She understood. Someone had knocked.

The door opened and a nice-looking couple in their early sixties entered.

Ethan's parents.

Marianna stood. "I'll give you some privacy."

He grabbed her hand. "Stay."

Curious looks from both newcomers sent her blushing, but she did her best to ignore it and smiled, holding out a hand. "Hello, I'm Marianna Santino."

"Liam and Margaret O'Hara." The big man who looked like an older version of Ethan gripped her hand in his. "Nice to meet you."

Ethan's mother nodded to Marianna, but her focus was clearly on the man in the bed.

Ethan blinked at the concern in his mother's eyes. He hadn't seen her in almost three months, since right around Thanksgiving when they'd informed him they'd be taking a monthlong cruise for the holidays.

Her fingers curled around his, and she said, "Oh Ethan, we were so worried. Are you all right?"

"Worried?"

Hurt flickered. "Of course. When a mother gets news that her son's been shot, she tends to worry a little."

"Like you worried about Ashley?"

The woman closed her eyes, took a deep breath. "We were wrong in the way we dealt with Ashley, Ethan. I'm so sorry. If we had it to do over again, we'd do it differently, oh, so differently."

He nearly fell out of the hospital bed. She was apologizing? Never before could he remember his mother saying she was sorry. He looked up at his father, stunned to see the man nodding. His dad swallowed hard and said, "After Ashley died, you kept yourself so aloof, so distant from us that we just figured you needed your space and time to deal with your grief the way you needed to. Unfortunately, that distance kept growing, and we've only just now come to understand that we should have done more, been there for you."

Shocked, Ethan's gaze darted between these strangers who were his blood relatives. "What made you come to that realization?"

"Your mom found Ashley's diary while cleaning up after Ashley...died. She wrote over and over about how she wanted us to come to know the Lord the way she did. She even wrote, 'Whatever it takes, Lord, whatever it takes.'"

Tears flowed freely. "How could we ignore what we decided was her dying wish? So, we started investigating the church and everything she held dear...and came to realize that God is who He says He is and we wanted to follow Him."

Marianna subtly placed a tissue box where Ethan's mother could reach it. The woman took a tissue, dabbed her eyes and gave an elegant sniff. Ethan sat stunned. Ashley's death had brought his parents to the saving love of Christ.

He wished it could have happened differently but knew Ashley wouldn't have had it any other way. She'd been on fire for her God, and it had brought about the results she wanted most. She'd made her mark on her world.

God had taken something horrible and used it for something wonderful. He closed his eyes and let the peace flow through him. *Thank you for the gift of forgiveness. I think I can finally forgive myself.*

Ethan opened his eyes and looked at Marianna noticing her tears. And felt love, peace and acceptance finally flow through him. God was good—always had been, always would be. Even in the midst of pain and heartache. Especially then.

His mother patted his hand and stood. "We'll go now. I hope you'll come home to our house to recuperate."

Ethan's eyes sought Marianna's, and she offered him a small smile and a nod. Her mother would understand. "Sure,

Mom, thanks." He cleared his throat but couldn't seem to get rid of the knot there. Then his parents were gone, and he held his hand out to Marianna.

"So, do you think you might want to go out with me?"

She met his eyes and grinned.

Simultaneously, they burst into laughter, Ethan wincing at the sting the motion produced, but ignoring it, willing to suffer anything in order to see her face creased with joy. Then she leaned down and planted her lips against his, and all was right with his world.

EPILOGUE

Four months later, Marianna packed the final box and stored it on the shelf. The last day of school had come and gone for the students, and today meant one more year of teaching under her belt. But that wasn't what had the excitement dancing within her. Ethan had promised her a drive up to the mountains of North Carolina.

Suddenly, warm hands covered hers and she jumped, startled but not scared. "I didn't hear you come in." A familiar wet nose nudged the bare calf not covered by the denim knee-length shorts she'd donned this morning. "You brought Twister!"

The hands fell away and he pulled her around to face him, once more allowing her the privilege of looking into his flashing blue eyes. She smiled, leaning forward to place a light kiss on his lips. He pulled her close for a squeeze then set her back. "Yep. I figured he might as well join us. He's a service dog and has the privilege of going anywhere we go. Now, you're the last one here except maintenance and security personnel. Are you ready to get going?"

"Definitely."

They'd planned to drive up tonight, tour Biltmore House, then have dinner in the main dining room. Ethan was going all out. Biltmore wasn't inexpensive. A new joy emanated from him, and Marianna reveled in it. Not that he would miss

Ashley in the years to come, but at least he'd finally made his peace with his sister's death. He was also well on his way to building a lasting, loving bond with his parents and Marianna thrilled at the fact that her own parents had grown to love this man as one of their own.

And he loved her.

She knew he did—his every action shouted it; he just hadn't said the words. But it would come. She just wished he would hurry up with it.

They left the building and climbed into his car, Twister settling himself into the backseat, tongue lolling from the side of his mouth. He'd recovered well.

Marianna silently said her goodbyes to the campus she wouldn't see until fall. Which was fine with her. As much as she loved her job, summer was the best perk the educational business offered.

Conversation flowed, yet underneath the easy words Marianna sensed an anticipation, an edginess about Ethan, and she wondered at it. They'd been on several day trips since he'd gotten out of the hospital and recovered, but this felt different. More exciting.

She shrugged. He'd tell her what was going on when he was ready.

The time flew and it seemed as if hardly any time had passed and they were already pulling into the gated grounds after a short stop to let Twister take care of his business. As they drove along the marked drive, they finally came to the spot to park. When Marianna opened the door, Twister bounded out and she snapped the leash on him and placed the badge on him that identified him as a service dog. Immediately, he settled into work mode and heeled by her left leg.

Ethan came around to take her right hand, and together the trio made their way to the large mansion just ahead.

After a whirlwind tour of the gorgeous interior, Ethan pulled Marianna into the gardens, which contained flowers in full bloom in every color imaginable. "What are you doing?"

She laughed at the sneaky look on his face. "Ethan, what are you up to?"

Finger held to his lips, he said, "Shush, follow me."

"But the tour's going that way."

"We're going to have our own tour—now are you with me?" Mischief glinted; his lips twitched to hold in a smile.

"You have a secret." Relenting, her heart racing at what she thought he might be up to, she gave in and followed him through the beautiful Azalea Garden, past the Walled Garden, and into the All-American Rose Garden. The flowers sprang forth, their rich colors surpassing anything she'd ever seen before, every hue, shape and shade. "Oh, Ethan, this is spectacular."

He took Twister's leash from her and dropped it. Twister would stay in that spot until someone picked up the leash handle and led him from it. Then Ethan pulled her close, looked into her eyes and there—with the sun shining down, the scent of roses in the air—said, "Marianna Santino, we've been through an awful lot. God has been so good to see that we've made it to this point. You are the most amazing woman I've ever met. You're loyal, kind, compassionate...."

The flush started up from her neck, and she knew her face would soon rival the red rose she could see over Ethan's shoulder. But there was no way she was going to stop him now. He pushed her hair back around her ear, his fingers grazing the hearing aid. She didn't even flinch. His right hand grasped her left. "Marianna, I know I don't deserve you, but I love you and want to know if you would do me the honor of being my wife?"

A circus of butterflies performed in her stomach, joy nearly caused her heart to explode, tears threatened to fall. She touched a finger to her hearing aid. "I'm bumping up the volume. I don't want to miss a word."

Amusement turned to outright humor, and he threw back his head to laugh. Twister cocked his head and perked his ears. Marianna grinned up at Ethan. "Why don't you repeat that last part to make sure I got it right?"

Laughter still rumbling, he pulled her in close and clamped his lips over hers for a kiss she'd never experienced before, one that left her breathless and yearning for a lifetime of his kisses. When he pulled back, the laughter still lingered, but love, passion and joy simmered in his eyes as well. "I said, you crazy woman, that I absolutely adore you. Will you marry me?"

This time she didn't bother to hold back the tears as she nodded and whispered, "Yes."

Ethan whooped and picked her up to swing in a circle, and Marianna clutched his shoulders, sheer joy running rampant through her. Finally, Ethan settled her back on her feet, kissed her one more time and said, "God is good, isn't He?"

"The best."

Then Ethan reached into his pocket and pulled out a small, square box. Her breath clogged her throat as he opened it and pulled out an exquisite pear-shaped diamond ring. With reverent gentleness, he slid it on the fourth finger of her left hand. A perfect fit.

"How did you know?"

He grinned. "Your mom helped me out."

"My mother knew about this?"

"Yep, your dad, too. I asked him before I asked you." Another grin slid across his lips. This time it had a bit of smugness to it.

Love filled her. She slid her arms around his neck. "You're incredible. I love you so much, Ethan O'Hara, and I thank God every day that you were there with me during that awful time a few months ago."

His eyes closed. "I never would have wished that time on you, but God brought us through it, taught me lessons I might never have otherwise learned…and bonded us together."

"For always."

"Till death do us part." He leaned down and claimed her lips one more time, sealing the promise to share in the loving, honoring and cherishing.

* * * * *

Dear Reader,

Thank you so much for joining me on Marianna and Ethan's journey. I used to work at our state school for the deaf located here in Spartanburg, South Carolina. Of course I drew upon my experiences there, but I promise, all the characters are completely products of my imagination, as are the activities that take place on the fictional campus.

I know so many wonderful deaf people and love deaf culture and the deaf world so much that I wanted to write about it. Marianna came from a large, protective family that would have allowed her to stay within their loving boundaries, but she was blessed with a streak of independence that enabled her to venture into the world without fear. However, she knew she had the comfort zone of her family to fall back on should she need it. And she did. She also knew God was the one who was going to have to rescue her and keep her safe. Fortunately, He chose to use Ethan to do it. I just love how God allows us to be a part of his master plan, don't you?

I think about this often. I want to make sure that I'm open to what the Lord wants to do with my life, and I pray you do, too!

Thank you again for reading *A Silent Terror*. I would love for you to e-mail me and let me know what you thought about it. You can reach me at lynetteeason.com. I always answer my e-mail personally and find great joy in meeting new people.

I look forward to hearing from you!

God bless,

Lynette Eason

DISCUSSION QUESTIONS

1. What do you think about Marianna's character? Do you like her? Is there anything you don't like about her?

2. What do you think about Ethan? Do you believe his fears about his ability to take care of Marianna are realistic when it comes to her being in danger?

3. Marianna stayed faithful to the God she loves. Ethan wondered if God cared. Which side of the fence are you on? When bad things happen, do you stick close to God or pull away?

4. Marianna comes from a big, loving family. Ethan comes from a family that needs to learn to communicate. Not everyone grows up in a loving Christian home. What kind of family do you come from, and are there things that you would change? What are they? Has God gotten you through some tough family times?

5. What was your favorite scene in the book, and why?

6. We all have life-changing experiences—good and bad. Think of an incident that changed your life, and, if you feel led, share what it was and how you dealt with it— good or bad.

7. There is a Scripture verse at the beginning of this book. Do you think it's appropriate for the story? Can you apply it to your own life? How?

8. What do you think about the use of a deaf/hearing-impaired woman as the main character? Did it bother you to find out she had a physical handicap?

9. Do you know any deaf people, and if so, what do you think about them, their language and culture? Or, if you don't, would you be interested in learning more as a result of this story?

10. What do you think about the secondary characters, such as Alonso, Marianna's younger brother? Was he a realistic character to you? Was his desire to help in the end believable?

11. Do you think Ethan and Marianna will have a happy future together? Do you think Ethan will find it hard not to smother Marianna and worry about her? Do you think he's "over" that?

12. Do you like the way the book ended? If so, why? If not, why not?

Turn the page for a sneak preview of bestselling author
Jillian Hart's novella
"Finally a Family."

One of two heartwarming stories celebrating motherhood
in
IN A MOTHER'S ARMS

On sale April 2009, only from
Steeple Hill Love Inspired Historical.

Chapter One

Montana Territory, 1884

Molly McKaslin sat in her rocking chair in her cozy little shanty with her favorite book in hand. The lush, new-spring green of the Montana prairie spread out before her like a painting, framed by the wooden window. The blue sky was without a single cloud to mar it. Lemony sunshine spilled over the land and across the open window's sill. The door was wedged open, letting the outside noises in—the snap of laundry on the clothesline and the chomping crunch of an animal grazing. My, it sounded terribly close.

The peaceful afternoon quiet shattered with a crash. She leaped to her feet to see her good—and only—china vase splintered on the newly washed wood floor. She stared in shock at the culprit standing at her other window. A golden cow with a white blaze down her face poked her head further across the sill. The bovine gave a woeful moo. One look told her this was the only animal in the yard.

"And just what are you doing out on your own?" She set her book aside.

The cow lowed again. She was a small heifer, still probably

more baby than adult. The cow lunged against the sill, straining toward the cookie racks on the table.

"At least I know how to catch you." She grabbed a cookie off the rack and the heifer's eyes widened. "I don't recognize you, so I don't think you belong here."

Molly skirted around the mess on the floor and headed toward the door. This was the consequence of agreeing to live in the country, when she had vowed never to do so again. But her path had led her to this opportunity, living on her cousin's land and helping the family. God had quite a sense of humor, indeed.

Before she could take two steps into the soft, lush grass surrounding her shanty, the cow came running, head down, big brown eyes fastened on the cookie. The ground shook.

Uh oh. Molly's heart skipped two beats.

"No, Sukie, no!" High, girlish voices carried on the wind.

Molly briefly caught sight of two identical school-aged girls racing down the long dirt road. The animal was too single-minded to respond. She pounded the final few yards, her gaze fixed on the cookie.

"Stop, Sukie. Whoa." Molly kept her voice low and kindly firm. She knew cows responded to kindness better than to anything else. She also knew they were not good at stopping, so she dropped the cookie on the ground and neatly stepped out of the way. The cow skidded well past the cookie and the place where Molly had been standing.

"It's right here." She showed the cow where the oatmeal treat was resting in the clean grass. While the animal backed up and nipped up the goody, Molly grabbed the cow's rope halter.

"Good. She didn't stomp you into bits." One of the girls said in serious relief. "She ran me over real good just last week."

"We thought you were a goner," the second girl said. "She's real nice, but she doesn't see very well."

"She sees well enough to have found me." Molly studied the girls. They both had identical black braids and golden-hazel eyes and fine-boned porcelain faces. One twin wore a green calico dress with matching sunbonnet, while the other wore blue. She recognized the girls from church and around town. "Aren't you the doctor's children?"

"Yep, that's us." The first girl offered a beaming, dimpled smile. "I'm Penelope and that's Prudence. We're real glad you found Sukie."

"We wouldn't want a cougar to get her."

"Or a bear."

What adorable children. A faint scattering of freckles dappled across their sun-kissed noses, and there was glint of trouble in their eyes as the twins looked at one another. The place in her soul thirsty for a child of her own ached painfully. She felt hollow and empty, as if her body would always remember carrying the baby she had lost. For one moment it was as if the wind died and the earth vanished.

"Hey, what is she eating?" One of the girls tumbled forward. "It smells like a cookie. You are a bad girl, Sukie."

"Did she walk into your house and eat off the counter?" Penelope wanted to know.

The grass crinkled beneath her feet as the cow tugged her toward the girls. "No, she went through the window."

Penelope went up on tiptoe. "I see them. They look real good."

Molly gazed down at their sweet and innocent faces. She wasn't fooled. Then again, she was a soft touch. "I'll see what I can do."

She headed back inside. "Do you girls need help getting the cow home?"

"No. She's real tame." Penelope and the cow trailed after her, hesitating outside the door. "We can lead her anywhere."

"Yeah, she only runs off when she's looking for us."

"Thank you so much, Mrs.—" Penelope took the napkin-wrapped stack of cookies. "We don't know your name."

"This is the McKaslin ranch," Prudence said thoughtfully. "But I know you're not Mrs. McKaslin."

"I'm the cousin. I moved here this last winter. You can call me Molly."

Penelope gave her twin a cookie. Beneath the brim of her sunbonnet, her face crinkled with serious thought. "You don't know our pa yet?"

"No, I only know Dr. Frost by reputation. I hear he's a fine doctor." That was all she knew. Of course she had seen his fancy black buggy speeding down the country roads at all hours. Sometimes she caught a brief sight of the man driving as the horse-drawn vehicle passed—an impression of a black Stetson, a strong granite profile and impressively wide shoulders.

Although she was on her own and free to marry, she paid little heed to eligible men. All she knew of Doctor Sam Frost was that he was a widower and a father and a faithful man, for he often appeared very serious in church. She reached through the open door to where her coats hung on wall pegs and worked the sash off her winter wool.

Prudence smiled. "Our pa's real nice and you make good cookies."

"And you're real pretty." Penelope was so excited she didn't notice Sukie stealing her cookie. "Do you like Pa?"

"I don't know the man, so I can't like him. I suppose I can't dislike him either." She bent to secure the sash around Sukie's halter. "Let me walk you girls across the road."

"You ought to come home with us." Penelope grinned. "Then you can meet Pa."

"Do you want to get married?" Penelope's feet were planted.

So were Prudence's. "Yes! You could marry Pa. Do you want to?"

"M-marry your pa?" Shock splashed over her like icy water.

"Sure. You could be our ma."

"And then Pa wouldn't be so lonely anymore."

Molly blinked. The words were starting to sink in. The

poor girls, wishing so much for a mother that they would take any stranger who was kind to them. "No, I certainly cannot marry a perfect stranger, but thank you for asking. I would take you two in a heartbeat."

"You would?" Penelope looked surprised. "Really?"

"We're an awful lot of trouble. Our housekeeper said that three times today since church."

"Does your pa know you propose on his behalf?"

"Now he does." A deep baritone answered. Dr. Frost marched into sight, rounding the corner of the shanty. His hat brim shaded his face, casting shadows across his chiseled features, giving him an even more imposing appearance. "Girls! Home! Not another word."

"But we had to save Sukie."

"She could have been eaten by a wolf."

Molly watched the good doctor's mouth twitch. She couldn't be sure, but a flash of humor could have twinkled in the depths of his eyes.

"You must be the cousin." He swept off his hat. The twinkle faded from his eyes and the hint of a grin from his lips. It was clear that while his daughters amused him, she did not. "I had no idea you would be so young."

"And pretty," Penelope, obviously the troublemaker, added mischievously.

Molly's face heated. The poor girl must need glasses. Although Molly was still young, time and sadness had made its mark on her. The imposing man had turned into granite as he faced her. Of course he had overheard his daughters' proposal, so that might explain it.

She smiled and took a step away from him. "Dr. Frost, I'm glad you found your daughters. I was about ready to bring them back to you."

"I'll save you the trouble." He didn't look happy. "Girls, take that cow home. I need to stay and apologize to Miss McKaslin."

She was a "Mrs.," but she didn't correct him. She had put

away her black dresses and her grief. Her marriage had mostly been a long string of broken dreams. She did better when she didn't remember. "Please don't be too hard on the girls on my behalf. Sukie's arrival livened up my day."

"At least there was no harm done." He winced. "There was harm? What happened?"

"I didn't say a word."

"No, but I could see it on your face."

Had he been watching her so closely? Or had she been so unguarded? Perhaps it was his closeness. She could see bronze flecks in his gold eyes, and smell the scents of soap and spring clinging to his shirt. A spark of awareness snapped within her like a candle newly lit. "It was a vase. Sukie knocked it off my windowsill when she tried to eat the flowers, but it was an accident."

"The girls should take better care of their pet." He drew his broad shoulders into an unyielding line. He turned to check on the twins, who were progressing down the road. The wind ruffled his dark hair. He seemed distant. Lost. "How much was the vase worth?"

How did she tell him it was without price? Perhaps it would be best not to open that door to her heart. "It was simply a vase."

"No, it was more." He stared at his hat clutched in both hands. "Was it a gift?"

"No, it was my mother's."

"And is she gone?"

"Yes."

"Then I cannot pay you its true value. I'm sorry." His gaze met hers with startling intimacy. Perhaps a door was open to his heart as well, because sadness tilted his eyes. He looked like a man with many regrets.

She knew well the weight of that burden. "Please, don't worry about it."

"The girls will replace it." His tone brooked no argument, but it wasn't harsh. "About what my daughters said to you."

"Do you mean their proposal? Don't worry. It's plain to see they are simply children longing for a mother's love."

"Thank you for understanding. Not many folks do."

"Maybe it's because I know something about longing. Life never turns out the way you plan it."

"No. Life can hand you more sorrow than you can carry." Although he did not move a muscle, he appeared changed. Stronger, somehow. Greater. "I'm sorry the girls troubled you, Miss McKaslin."

Mrs., but again she didn't correct him. It was the sorrow she carried that stopped her from it. She preferred to stand in the present with sunlight on her face. "It was a pleasure, Dr. Frost. What blessings you have in those girls."

"That I know." He tipped his hat to her, perhaps a nod of respect, and left her alone with the restless wind and the door still open in her heart.

* * * * *

Don't miss IN A MOTHER'S ARMS
Featuring two brand-new novellas from bestselling authors
Jillian Hart and Victoria Bylin.
Available April 2009
from Steeple Hill Love Inspired Historical.

And be sure to look for SPRING CREEK BRIDE
by Janice Thompson,
also available in April 2009.

REQUEST YOUR FREE BOOKS!

2 FREE RIVETING INSPIRATIONAL NOVELS
PLUS 2 FREE MYSTERY GIFTS

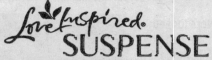

YES! Please send me 2 FREE Love Inspired® Suspense novels and my 2 FREE mystery gifts (gifts are worth about $10). After receiving them, if I don't wish to receive any more books, I can return the shipping statement marked "cancel". If I don't cancel, I will receive 4 brand-new novels every month and be billed just $4.24 per book in the U.S. or $4.74 per book in Canada, plus 25¢ shipping and handling per book and applicable taxes, if any*. That's a savings of over 20% off the cover price! I understand that accepting the 2 free books and gifts places me under no obligation to buy anything. I can always return a shipment and cancel at any time. Even if I never buy another book, the two free books and gifts are mine to keep forever.

123 IDN ERXX 323 IDN ERXM

Name	(PLEASE PRINT)	
Address		Apt. #
City	State/Prov.	Zip/Postal Code

Signature (if under 18, a parent or guardian must sign)

Order online at www.LoveInspiredSuspense.com
Or mail to Steeple Hill Reader Service:

IN U.S.A.: P.O. Box 1867, Buffalo, NY 14240-1867
IN CANADA: P.O. Box 609, Fort Erie, Ontario L2A 5X3

Not valid to current subscribers of Love Inspired Suspense books.

Want to try two free books from another series?
Call 1-800-873-8635 or visit www.morefreebooks.com

* Terms and prices subject to change without notice. N.Y. residents add applicable sales tax. Canadian residents will be charged applicable provincial taxes and GST. Offer not valid in Quebec. This offer is limited to one order per household. All orders subject to approval. Credit or debit balances in a customer's account(s) may be offset by any other outstanding balance owed by or to the customer. Please allow 4 to 6 weeks for delivery. Offer available while quantities last.

Your Privacy: Steeple Hill Books is committed to protecting your privacy. Our Privacy Policy is available online at www.SteepleHill.com or upon request from the Reader Service. From time to time we make our lists of customers available to reputable third parties who may have a product or service of interest to you. If you would prefer we not share your name and address, please check here. ☐

LISUS08R

Love Inspired
SUSPENSE

TITLES AVAILABLE NEXT MONTH

On sale April 14, 2009

CODE OF HONOR by Lenora Worth
Get in, save the girl and get back out. CHAIM agent
Brice Whelan's agenda seems foolproof...until he tries
to rescue missionary/nurse Selena Carter. When danger
follows Selena home, Brice has to protect her, which means
sticking by her side—whether she wants him there or not.

CLOUD OF SUSPICION by Patricia Davids
Without a Trace

Leather-jacketed rebel Patrick Rivers has always had a
bad reputation. And now that he's back in town to settle
his stepfather's estate, Patrick knows he isn't welcome.
But the chance to keep Shelby Mason safe could be reason
enough to stay.

MURDER AT EAGLE SUMMIT by Virginia Smith
A body found on the slopes turns the wedding guests at
Eagle Summit ski resort into suspects. Liz Carmichael might
be a witness, so she files a police report...with her ex-fiancé,
Deputy Tim Richards. After three years apart, she can
finally make things right—unless the killer finds her first.

SHADOWS ON THE RIVER by Linda Hall
Ally Roarke was fourteen when she witnessed a murder...
and was forced out of town by the teenage killer's
prominent parents. Years later, the killer is a respected
businessman. And Ally, now a single mom, can't let the past
go. Especially when there's another death close to home.

LISCNMBPA0309